HILLSOUNDS

· T H R E E ·

*A collection of poems, prose and tall tales
from the members of the
Writers, Readers and Poets Society
of Brown County, Indiana*

Other books by W.R.A.P.S.

Hillsounds (1997)

Hillsounds, Volume 2 (1998)

ISBN-13: 978-0-9852257-4-2 (paperback)
ISBN-13: 978-0-9852257-5-9 (e-book)

First Edition

W.R.A.P.S. –
Writers, Readers and Poets Society
PO Box 2144 · Nashville, Indiana 47448

Memoria

This book is in memory of
Betty Ann Moebs
1942 – 2012

*Betty was a W.R.A.P.S. member for only two years, but
we carry with us unforgettable memories of her faith, her
devotion to her family, and her love of nature, especially
animals. Her writing is included in* Hillsounds Three *as a
living monument to Betty's talent, creativity and energy.*

Contents

Authors

Dedication

Hill Sounds III would not exist if two particular men living in Brown County, Indiana had not come together to form a group they named Writers, Readers and Poets Society of Brown County. This group has been a haven of sorts for hundreds of people, from all walks of life and all age levels, who wanted to try putting their thoughts down on paper then share their compositions in a safe friendly setting with other writers of varying backgrounds and writing experience.

For nearly two a decades, at least twice a month, all of these writers were welcomed by a rather odd duo…a loud country farmer turned painter and writer, who loved to chew tobacco and spit out profanity, and a gentle very soft spoken Quaker pacifist, who turned native timber into works of art that many residents now call home. Some writers came to only one meeting which was all that was required from the beginning to become an official member. Many other writers have attended sporadically and yet a few others are almost religious about their attendance. One person especially, stands out in the "religious" category.

This book is dedicated by the members of W.R.A.P.S. to these very different and very remarkable Brown County men who founded our group, the late Von Williamson and the still breathing Hank Swain, with deep gratitude and appreciation for their dedication to us and to our beloved Brown County community. It is also dedicated to Keith Bradway for his "religious" attendance and his impeccable attention to the details that keeps a group like ours going.

— *Susan W. Showalter*

Foreword

by Keith Bradway

The Writers, Readers, and Poets Society (W.R.A.P.S.) was established in 1995; it published *Hill Sounds* in 1997 and *Hill Sounds II* in 1998. You may wonder why it has taken fourteen years to publish again. It was difficult to find someone to take on the burden of editor. Levi Thomas, the editor of *Hill Sounds,* had developed other interests and no longer participated. Paul and Becky McCreary, editors of *Hill Sounds II,* moved to New Mexico and were not available. Our members have supplanted such joint efforts by publishing on their own. They included Von Williamson (before his death in 2005), Hank Swain, Carolyn Griffin, Tricia Bock, Paul Shriver, Deb Bowden, Susan Showalter, Patience Northern, Deborah Cronin, John Sisson, and Debi Hurt.

The group has pursued its literary purpose in other ways. Hank Swain started a Tall Tales Contest in 2004. It was an annual affair for four years, but it then stopped for lack of interest. It resumed in 2012.

The group sponsored Writers' Conferences in 2009 and 2010 managed by Debi Hurt. Forty aspiring writers attended each event.

What we present has been influenced and enriched by the hundreds of members who joined us over our seventeen years. The authors of this book have a wide range of ages and backgrounds. Their contributions cover a variety of types of prose and poetry. We think your time with it will be well rewarded.

ALLISON DISTLER

Allison is an introspective non-fiction writer and poet who maintains her own blog and enjoys combining written word with visual form. She comes from a background in singing, song writing, and performing, and is curious about cultivating intimate relationships between voice, expression, intuition, and artistic mediums. She is on the faculty of Women Writing for (a) Change Bloomington and currently teaches with the young women's program for girls in grades 4-6. You can read more of her ongoing stories at www.theharmonioushome.net/blog.

Ask Me

Ask me if I am a mystic
I will point to the tree,
The one
 in the middle
of vast field space-
where the horse goes for shade
and lightening is drawn

Ask me if I am a mystic
I'll show you the silo
Navy, sinking in the black soil
the crumbled hog barn…
I'll make a run to the cattle fence,
startling them
and glide on the white
chipped porch swing

Ask me if I am a mystic
I'll lift the cover to the ground well,
unlatch the wood shed
and climb the ladder
past the rusty tractor
to the family of kittens born in the hay

Ask me if I am a mystic
as the storm rolls in
wiping out the purple sky,
bending tall emerald stalks
inspiring miles of corn tassels dancing
shifting the air from water to ether.

When lightening strikes the tip
of the paint brush tree
Ask me.

The Backyard Circus

It started with the backyard circus
And the neighborhood hikes
The second grade secret club
The ten year old dance troupe

It started with my brother,
An August birth
being left out,
a broken heart
looking down
undoubtedly alone
feeling — not wanted,
scooting gravel with the toe of a sandal

A little girl's revenge

It started with the backyard circus

Conviction, selling tickets
To anyone who wandered

Souls on the wayside

A secret language

For those seeking something other
being summoned, to come
past the bitter habit,
of solitary promise

If I was left out,
there must be others.

Being Held

All the wet mouths of
tight pant lovers
can keep dripping
while I vision one more moon
at the fire with you

Our hands
steady, gentle safe for me to place any place without
worry — a shoulder, thigh…
Safe enough to mold a face cradle and cry

Here, I am strong and feel able to allow myself to be
contained in you
safe for me to place my trust in man, a vessel.

Indiana, January 5:17 PM

Crows fly drunk
towards gnarled frames
To perch on stark branches.

Totems on painted veins
in the powdered blue canvas
of winter's remains

TRICIA BOCK

Tricia Bock lives in the village of Nashville. She is a poet and this fact is often painfully obvious. She has published two books of her own and has been lucky enough to be included in both prior Hill Sounds books published by W.R.A.P.S.. For all these things, she is grateful.

And Winter Finally Comes...

etching with soft lines the frost on the window pane
freezing the birds bathing place
encrusting branches in glittering ice

People rush to buy bread and milk
as if bread and milk would save them
in their energy efficient electric homes
sealed tight from nature,
but with no alternative heat source

I prefer my drafty old house
the wood stoves are blazing today
nice and warm and with a flat top
perfect for making homemade soup

Light the candles or old glass lamps
(we now have oil for the job,
as we are so modern, these days)
but still the light is enough to read by
which is all that really matters

The cat gets lazier,
lying behind the stove
curled and dreaming of mouse laden fields
the smells and sounds of summer
busy in his head

I have a good book to read, a waning full moon,
    a warm hearth,
and all I could ever really need.

Sword Play / Sword Rest

Lazy days in the pavilion, soft blankets below, soft blue skies above
    the smells of cook fires and lavender,
    the warmth of the sun as it heats the side of the pavilion walls,
    the wind gently causing them to move
    in and out like the sail of a boat,
    gliding on quiet water with the surface of glass.

We sit, with paper and quill in hand,and glasses of mead cooled by
    earthenware cups and write of the challenges of the day,
    the clash of skill and strategy.

We reminisce of days and warriors and others we have known,
    and of battles yet to be fought; smiles on our faces at these
    prospects.

Staffs and swords lie nearby, the never ending practice session just
    around a corner.

Pillows for rest and tomes of new methods for war are ever present.

Occasional conversation and laughter is a standard as well, as is the
    solving of the world's problems under this tent.

These are the days of summer, followed by
    those famous summer nights
    bonfires and battle, ladies in camp finery,
    mead flowing like water.

Our companions, tried and true by fire and ice,
    all gather as night comes.

Stories are read, tales of bravery and honor and life,
    and we know all is well.

Mark these days, good sirs, for they will not pass again.
    There is no second chance for memory making at the Pavilion.

But we are of the kind who live every moment we are alive,
    so this warning is truly unwarranted, for souls like ours that burn
    with a clear, true flame.

In the Moment

To let go of the things that were—
for they cloud up the mind that is.

To let go of the things to come—
for they never were reality.

To let go of the "if only I had"—
because you simply 'did' and now it is 'done.'

To let go of the "what ifs"—
for dreams belong in sleep, not in the moment.

To let go of any of these is difficult—
but freedom is never the easy path.

But to let go of these things,
that never were real to begin with—
is to be truly free.

BETTY MOEBS

Betty Moebs worked as a chaplain and teacher in a variety of settings and late in life taught an early childhood education class online for Ivy Tech Community College. She had a passion for writing, especially poetry, journaling, and song parodies. She gave workshops and retreats on journaling and published a children's book, *Don't Tickle My Pits,* and a meditation CD, *On the Barge.* Betty also wrote a column for *Pen It!* Magazine called "Picture Prompts" and served on the Brown County Community Foundation and Scholarship Committee.

Betty was born in and grew up in Chicago, where she met her husband Dave. They moved to Indianapolis where they raised their five children. In late live they lived in Brown County where they enjoyed visitors, especially their 13 grandchildren who were entertained by the lake and nature's feathered and furry creatures.

Dancing Lights

I stood in front of Annie's grave and wondered where the time had gone since I saw her in a coma ten years before. She was in the infirmary, close to death when I visited. I had stayed, telling her about my Great Books 6th grade campers and about seeing the faceless nun. Annie would have known the story of the faceless nun, the legend of a nun who roamed the campus to keep her spirit alive because the artist commissioned to paint her portrait died before he finished her face. What Annie didn't know was that each week, during the final campfire, a counselor told the story under the eerie shadows cast by the moon in the woods. After the campfire had dimmed to embers, another counselor, dressed in a black habit and screen-meshed face, moved silently around the campfire, totally spooking the gullible campers.

As I stood at Annie's grave, I wondered what became of the thirteen bright campers I had directed that week. I wondered how long their innocence kept alive what they believed about the faceless nun. And I remembered how the silence in the infirmary room had been broken by Annie's labored breathing. I remembered thinking how cold her hand was and how she had pulled it away when I leaned over to kiss her good-bye and how she motioned for me to draw nearer. She had opened her eyes and whispered, "What are the children reading this week?"

"I have told so many people that story, Annie," I said, as much to the wind as to the tombstone in front of me, shivers running up my arms and tears rolling down my cheeks. I felt my feet, cold and damp from the dew, and when I looked down I noticed twinkling lights by Annie's grave.

Were those insects in front of my feet? I froze. I was mesmerized by the dancing lights. What kind of insects were they? I had never seen them before. I didn't want to scare them away, so I just stood there, trying not to move. My curiosity grew. I had to lean forward to see. Nothing around me moved. And I realized that I wasn't seeing insects at all. It was the morning dew glistening on blades of grass. I was looking at prisms of nature sparkling in the sunlight of early dawn.

I left the cemetery and returned to the conference center to join participants for the final session of the conference. But I couldn't concentrate. The speaker had been wonderful. I had heard Jack Shay before - read his books - listened to his tapes. But this morning my mind was back in the cemetery, engrossed by the puzzle of the dancing lights. Everyone in my family had been campers. When we went camping, I had often gotten up early in the morning to walk. I loved listening to the sounds and marveling at nature bringing in the new day. How many times had I walked at dawn? We had gone camping dozens of times over the years. Maybe I slept in some mornings. Maybe I was drawn to look for critters. Maybe there were times when one of more of the kids walked with me and I was distracted. But I should have seen the prism lights many, many times when I walked. But I hadn't. Why not? I sat there wondering.

My mind wandered to other images – the commissioning ceremony the night before when gentle hands dried my feet as part of the commissioning ritual of the washing of feet. I was now a Minister of Providence because I had been commissioned. My thoughts were a curious collage of years ago and the night before, of books and papers, my pastoral project, the qualifying exam, exams and lectures, of people I met, people I had grown to know and love. I was thinking about and wondering where it would all lead me.

My mind drifted back to the lecture hall when I heard someone ask Shea, ""Did the apostles know who Jesus was and what He was all about?" The answer I heard made a lasting impression. "No, the disciples didn't have a clue about Jesus or what he was all about – until they were commissioned – and then they saw the light."

Christmas Re-discovered

"Whatever possessed you to hide in this closet?" That question ran through my mind as I started shivering while crouched behind boxes in the unheated closet — a 10' long x 4' wide x 4' high closet that formed "eaves" in our cape cod home. I just wanted to not be the first — or second — one found again. In the first round, I was the first one found, given away by our cat meowing in front of the door behind which I was hiding. And I was the second one found when, after hearing one of the lookers say, "mom can't be back there, it's too small," and I giggled, giving away my secret.

But now it was really getting cold. I had seen the light twice when the lookers opened the closet door and scanned the boxes, strewn randomly on the floor. They shut the door, dismissing any possibility that anyone could be in the back. I could cough, or let out a little squeal and surely I would be found. But I didn't want to. This was just too much fun. I couldn't remember when the seven of us had played hide-and-go-seek in the house.

It had all started when I had asked the two oldest to ask the restaurant where they both worked to assign them the same shift on Christmas (I didn't want to draw straws again to see who wasn't going to eat with the family). Because they both voiced their discomfort, I brought a politely written request to their supervisor. Thank you, Lord! The kids worked the first shift and got home early enough so that we could eat before three — giving grandma and grandpa time to be able to drive home while it was still light out. We were faced with how to use the time we had on Christmas for the first time in years. Television was not an option — my rule. Most of our board games worked for the older kids, but not the youngest who were five and seven. I wanted them to choose but hoped the choice would be acceptable to everyone. Our oldest daughter asked, "What about Hide and Seek?"

The loud "yes" was unanimous. The timing, age-wise, was perfect because our youngest was still little enough to be stuffed into a clothes hamper, the blanket chest, and one of the boxes that earlier in the day bore the contents of a Christmas present. He was in seventh heaven!

And the "stuffers" and "hiders" and "cover-uppers" were enjoying it just as much as he was.

After being the first or second one found in the rounds we had already played, I could tell by their voices that I was the only left to be found. I heard someone say, "the basement" and as the voices dimmed, I knew it would be quiet again as they all searched the rooms two floors below me. I knew I could stretch and wiggle and shake my one leg that was now falling asleep and not get caught. I had just finished getting comfortable again, though cold, when I heard what sounded like elephant feet on the stairs. I knew I couldn't last much longer, but I didn't want to give myself away.

And then it came to me. I wondered if that is how Jesus feels at Christmas — wanting us to re-discover Him again at Christmas, but not wanting to force Himself on us. I imagined that He wants us to celebrate. I imagined Him rejoicing with us in seeking the baby who wants to be born again in our hearts. I imagined His wanting us to hear the choir and perceive that we're hearing angels singing, and to see in the crib the gift of love that awaits all who believe.

Yes, that was my favorite remembered Christmas!

Winter Ambiance

Pregnant lurking 'neath a midnight sky
on cloudless night of stars

This moonlit scene does hint
 through snow-kissed branches now silent
a collage of tracks on snow betraying winter's mantra
softly echoed in some distant not quite hidden movement
and marked above the ice and white of lake
that frames a timeless din of ambivalent shadows of shapes
suggesting some unknown legacy until dawn does break
renewing images of the pilgrimage repeated

Halloween

Up the steps the spotted leopard tiptoed
with black caped cackler wearing pointed hat
Their outstretched hands were already stickied
when they rang the bell squealing "trick or treat"

Their faces were red-hued from suckers lick-ied
tired — they — from walking way down the street
where they saw skinny Flat Stanley who was flat
from laying on the grass when it got mowed!

Dusk

Dusk is an interim, a time where light does hint
at what is past and is what is yet to come
It teases, casting shadows ominous
that magnify all fears
of evils remembered from a near or distant past

Then hope enters in to dwell as shapes and hues
become conjured witnesses to transition subtle
For what emerges is not only light that's fading
but truth – real or faux
and a place in time

too short for eye of mind to dwell on
but enough to wonder if this interim
'tween yesterday and kairos yet to come
is hint of more than what the eye can see

The Water's Edge

I must go down to the water's edge
    to feel the waves pressing my toes
    into the rippled wet sand
    and hear the ritual mantra
    in harmony with the ebb and flow
    lulling me at the water's edge

I must go down to the water's edge
    to hear the bull frogs echoing
    with their drum-like staccato "rivet"
    and feel the beating of their ritual song
    in harmony with trees swaying in the breeze
    mesmerizing me at the water's edge

I must go down to the water's edge
    to drink in sights and textures and sounds
    of nature's gifts from my vantage point
    and see winged and furry critters in a ritual dance
    in harmony with fishes in and
    white caps on the lake
    calming me at the water's edge

I must go down to the water's edge
    to see and feel and hear and celebrate
    oblivious of time - aware only of being present
    where memories blend in a collage of yesterdays
    in harmony with all that is and is in the moment
    embracing me at the water's edge

Oops!

Did you ever hear the label, "Technology challenged?"
Well, more than an understatement, that's a joke
If I were getting paid to work a "help desk" job
you'll soon find out why I'd be broke

I know how to highlight and how to paginate
and move words around and change the font or the type size
I can underline and *italicize* and make a word look **bold**
but trying to remember what's in a file or folder I despise

Just the sound of the words to me are intimidating
my brain turns to mush and I don't have a clue
I get stressed out just looking at too many icons on the screen
and the mouse sometimes has an agenda it wants to pursue

So listen to what happened as I sat at my computer on my desk
composing and editing several pages I needed to save
I had begun the process of moving the arrow "thingamajing"
to click on "file" and scroll down — but it didn't behave

And then all in a flash I witnessed what I think was a "melt down"
and I screamed (uncharacteristically) and went into a rage
because somehow — and I don't really know how it happened —
I pressed the wrong key and I deleted every last page!

Finger Dreams

It was just the right height to be seen
 On a shelf with other pastels where it lay
 Snuggled next to a floppy-eared bunny
 Was a cute little lamb that didn't baaaa

Oh! t'was too too much for little hands to suppress
 When in her head she heard a "please touch me"
 so with outstretched arms she lifted the little lamb
 while dreams danced in the head of this child of three

She looked so lovingly — first at it — and then at me
 while pressing the little lamb close to her heart
 and I wondered whether, when our table was called,
 with this chosen stuffed animal she'd be able to part

She then lowered her head and gently placed the lamb
 In a nest made by moving the other animals all 'round
 And as she continued her looking with longing eyes
 I thought "what a softie" in grandma she's found

She took a step back from the bin on the shelf
 After stroking the lamb with her fingers once more
 Then closing her eyes she smiled and put in her treasure chest
 The memory of a lamb she met in the Cracker Barrel store

On Winged and Furry Creatures – Haiku

See chipmunks darting
   in a random ritual
   entertainers faux

A yellow finch sings
   its beauty mesmerizes
   stay on feeder, please

Puffy-cheeked squirrel
   runs circles up and down trees
   bushy-tailed culprit

Red headed 'pecker
   discarding your seed droppings
   you are arrogant

In shadows he lurks
   looking for scraps at midnight
   did I say Raccoon?

SUSAN W. SHOWALTER

Susan's childhood memories include "helping" in the press room owned by her grandfather, Ernest W. Showalter, a newspaper publisher in Brookville, IN. Several of her family members have been successful professional writers…perhaps writing is in her blood!

She began writing and taking pictures professionally in Columbus, IN for *The Evening Republican* newspaper when she was 17 years old then studied Journalism at Indiana University in Bloomington, IN before changing to an Apparel Design Major at The Fashion Institute of Technology, S.U.N.Y. Following graduation in 1968 in NYC on the stage at Carnegie Hall, Susan worked as a designer in San Francisco, Toronto and Europe.

Returning to Indiana in 1970, she made leather goods, candles, designer jewelry, quilts and hand-made art papers in Brown County. After surviving debilitating spine and neck injuries in 1998, Susan returned to newspaper and magazine writing.

Working as a fine art landscape photographer, she traveled to Egypt, China and Mexico and has received state and federal grants to produce documentaries. Her present passion is interviewing and writing about artists and musicians. Susan also writes about environmental issues and reflects on her life in Brown County where she lives in a 109 acre forest preserve. She won an award in 2011 from The Indiana Society of Professional Journalists for contributions to the radio show, *The Brown County Hour.*

W.R.A.P.S. members inspired Susan to try creative writing. She founded Brown County Poets Agains the War in 2002 and her poems were included in an international collection, *Poets Agains the War,* which was presented to the U.S. Congress in 2003. Her work may be viewed at Handmade in Brown County Gallery near Nashville, IN or by visiting her website at www.HandmadeinBrownCounty.com.

Another Goat Hill Spring

Steep, deeply rutted driveway,
etched by days and nights of driving spring rains,
provides an excuse to stay home…
to rest from last week's unexpected excitement
an unexpected house guest,
a highly successful art exhibition,
an unexpected trip to Indianapolis,
for an unexpected journalism award,
followed by that unexpected sleepless night
interrupted with unexpected frantic calls
from my concerned daughter
warning me of a tornado
then urging me into the closet downstairs.

Being at home the past three days
causes me to yearn for the early days.
Some 40 years ago,
here on Goat Hill,
I hardly ever left this place.

Then we grew and canned our food,
milked twenty some goats,
cared for horses, dogs, cats, chickens, geese,
cut firewood for cooking
and to heat the house and water.
We made our own entertainment
using a banjo, dulcimer and two voices,
sharing meals with friends.
There was no electronic intruder…
just a radio
plugged into the car battery.
Life was simple, fun
and more direct.

I enjoy spring rains affecting everything.
Tree leaves quadruple in size each day.
Forest transcends from black and browns
to green and bright blossoms everywhere!

Friends, family
after nearly 40 years,
do not understand
my need to be here.
They cannot comprehend
the deep love I have
for my very natural remote home,
the serenity I feel here.
They also cannot comprehend
their approval is not required.

This place and I have enjoyed
a long marriage.
Sometimes I get lonely.
Most of the time
I am lost
in beauty here
in sweet memories
of artists friends,
lovers long gone now.
These memories,
this love,
are part of this place…
they are part of me.

Out of the Blue

Warm bright February sky, insisting it is spring, bounds through southern windows into my kitchen and living room. Dancing to some favorite music from Lou Stant's CD, *"Out of the Blue"*, I waltz between these rooms and the laundry room toying with routine tasks which keep the household functioning.

What an appropriate name, I think. It seems as if it were just chosen for this day! What a way to get these jobs done! I love this very original CD which really "struts its stuff" showing off Lou's broad talents as a writer and musician. Some of the songs are really funny. Others, deep and gentle, remind me of Lenard Cohen.

The dancing stops from time to time, to concentrate on words, to listen to the music and to notice birds at the feeder outside the kitchen window. Later, dancing takes a longer pause…I'm spending time on the phone with Kurt Young talking lawyer stuff and, most importantly, finding out about his next gig. He'll be at the Abe Martin Lodge to-morrow night with his wife Marge, "sitting in" for the remarkable Kara Barnard who will most likely be doing a gig somewhere else or per-forming out of the state in a music studio backing up someone else's CD.

Kara is accomplished on thirteen instruments, including the saw. Many have found that it is financially much more efficient to hire her for back up work than to hire several musicians who can each play only one or two instruments. This keeps Kara very busy and away from her be-loved cabin here. I promise Kurt I'll try to make it tomorrow night. I ad-mit that I have even bought a park pass, to avoid the usual gate fee, mak-ing the weekly trips into the park for these Saturday night gigs affordable.

Keeping my dreams alive, we also talk of reviving Brown County Earth Day and plans for the Brown County Music Guild. I quiz Kurt about this and that… "What dates would be good? At the court house, or at the Village Green?" I take notes to remember his preferences. Then, icing on the conversation…we discuss a not so far fetched dream about getting a building downtown Nashville where the not yet organized music guild could have a coffee house complete with local performing musicians, local writers reading their recent works, rooms for giving music lessons and even a recording studio! This would all be part of a not-for-profit educational organization run by the member artists.

These dreams of mine, born one night at The Daily Grind, are getting old but they are not getting stale. I get fed encouragement and excitement when I talk to my musician friends about them but, also always, this is accompanied by some concerned comments about them not wanting to be part of the work of organizing it. I assure them all that is OK because that is the part I love.

"You write, play and teach the music," I always tell them. "The rest will take care of itself." Of course, I think to myself, I was much younger and much healthier in 1978 when I started the Brown County Craft Guild and Gallery. Of course, I keep this negative thought to myself.

I check in by phone with writer friends Pete Sebert and Von Williamson welcoming the report that Von is doing better. I ask if he is getting enough to eat. I ask, just like the mother that I am. My call was to make an offer to take Von for a ride. Maybe I'd take him down Highway 135 South to where he lived on his farm while he was still painting and breathing much easier when I showed up in Brown County in 1972, but I do not make that offer. Hearing Von is unable to get outside and sensing my reports of the beautiful day are making him feel worse because he isn't out enjoying it, I decide to leave that offer for another sunny day.

I dance and chores pause again. I talk with Chris Webb, checking out the timeframe for Pat's gig on Sunday down at the Story Bar and Grill. I'll be inviting friends, even offering food, trying to get them to come from Columbus, Hayden and from Indy for these events so I need to get the time right. Chris, as usual, will be performing with his Pop as will Mack Jump, from Indy.

The month old uncompleted painting job on my bedroom ceiling lures me upstairs. I try to walk by the computer but cannot resist sitting down then send invitations to these upcoming musical events. Pictures, which I took at the "Rally for America" (held after the 9/11 events at the 4H fairgrounds) and at The Brown County Singer Songwriter Showcase in November at Mike's Dance Barn, are also sent to Kurt. Brown County musicians have become favorite subjects as I try to master the digital camera.

Guilt, coming from the bedroom ceiling, somehow disappears as I take some time to write about my day. I feel my usual joy about living in Brown County and wish I could express what I feel with words. I am blessed to live with so many creative people and, of course, with all the beauty surrounding us. The way I feel about the physical beauty here cannot be described better than my writer and geologist friend, Jonathon Thompson of Kentucky, has recently written in his online journal:

"...and this is what I call my homeland...my affinity with this land is well beyond the mere choice of lifestyles — beyond the choice of geography. These lands here have a spell on my heart and soul — so when I gaze at some spectacle, there are things beyond the vision....things beyond any sense of physical or temporal coordinates — the land very certainly has its own spirit — and when I extend myself —my own spirit, we are entwined —what I see with my eyes, hear with my ears, smell with my nose are at the surface — there is something magnificently deeper about my homeland — so deep, I don't suppose I'll ever fathom its complete meaning or envision it entirely.

I read a scientific paper recently suggesting that the human mind endears itself to a relatively small geography in an individual's lifetime. I have sensed this — moving an hour in any direction from Richards Bend, the land changes to the east and south, it become more mountainous — to the north and west, more rolling, or even flat. But the feel of the land is what is so striking -how totally different it feels to me...It is hard for me to imagine that most human beings don't consider, at all, their own geography — not for jobs changes, not for choice of home-towns... it is hard for me to imagine not being spiritually connected to a land — it is hard for me to imagine not being spiritually contiguous with my homeland."

(*Richard's Bend Journal,* Until the Hepatica Bloom, *by Jonathon Thompson, Feb. 2, 2002, pg. 27.*)

Maybe, someday, I will be lucky enough to show Jonathon around Brown County. Maybe someday I will be lucky enough to meet this talented gentle sensitive man. I feel that same affinity for the land here in Brown County. I feel it for the creative people who live here now and have in the past...the writers, the painters, the craftspeople, and the musicians. They fill me up, they keep me warm and they keep me sane. I sense that many, many others here feel the same. We have bonded to this land here and we have bonded to each other.

Mills Pots

Saw John the potter
He was in his new pot shop
It felt like old times

I eat off Mills pots
The food tastes a lot better
The price was right too

Pots were wedding gifts
Helped us celebrate our life
When marriage was good

Pots still beautiful
Sturdy in more ways than one
Survived that marriage

I talk to those pots
They listen, smile knowingly
They are like old friends

Got mad at the pots
Thought about throwing them out
When John left Maggie

But like real true friends ‑
Those pots, I share meals again
We got over it

My kid wants the pots
When I am dead and long gone
They will feed her too —

Late Life Crisis

Her young life had touched a young man's.
He had come to train community organizers
of which she was one.
This migrant workers' son,
this professionals' daughter
shared passions about their work
and respect for each other.
They bonded quickly.

He played his guitar for her,
sang to her in Spanish and English.
He took her to visit his cousins
at a nearby migrant camp.
Opening concerts for Joan Baez and the like,
he had been a professional musician
who had given all that up to fight
for the migrant workers' rights.
Together they led a protest
in the Office of Economic Opportunity
when she had last seen him in Chicago.

February, 33 years later on his birthday,
he abruptly appeared
peering out of an announcement
on her computer screen in her bedroom!
She recognized his eyes-
dark thick hair had thinned,
young smooth face now creased,
But, oh, those eyes!
He is a speaker at the Dennis Kucinich
Queen City event
she planned to attend.
Squealing with delight,
she sent him an email.

Warm smiling eyes greeted hers
as he rose to his feet to embrace her.
Encircling her with large smiles,
they became twenty-three again
floating above the noisy crowd!

His speech felt like an old friend.
He told of the migrant workers' struggle,
invited listeners into action,
asked people to work for change.
Old passions stirred in her wet eyes.

Five hours after he scrawled
a Spanish message on her new CD,
the woman climbed alone
up her dark icy hillside in the next state.
Falling in darkness, she firmly told herself
she must get up and move on!
She did just that.

She lay all night listening, crying
as her dear old friend's beautiful music
filled her heart and bedroom.
She was grieving losses
long gone youth
long gone loves.
time spent on unimportant things…
She knew the excruciating truth:
she had not lived the meaningful life
she had always hoped to live.

Through his music,
he appeared in her bedroom again.
She recognized his eyes-
dark thick hair had thinned,
young smooth face now creased was wiser,
and, oh, those eyes!
The warmth in his voice soothed her…
he invited her into action,
he asked her to work for change.

The Day the Queen
Tried to Silence the Poets

Come to my house, The White House.
Let's have tea, let's party.
Let's call it "Poetry and the American Voice."
Let's honor Dickinson, Whitman and Hughes

But remember, I am the Queen!
You must obey my rules:
You must pretend the awful things happening aren't!
You must speak only words that I want to hear.

Queen Laura sent her invitation to an elite few.
Some thought they would come
Add feathers to their caps
But some of the others thought better of that

You see, poets must speak words
That must be spoken.
These poets said "No!",
They would not go!

Queen Laura got word
The elite of the elite
Planned to stoop to using
Freedom of speech!

As the Queen wondered,
"Who do they think they are?"
She canceled "Poetry and the American Voice"
To silence all the poets near and far.

But these poets knew that Queens cannot silence poets
That it's better to not even try to.
These poets knew
They had important work to do.

Faster than Emily, Langston and Walt
Could turn over in their graves
Poets the world over organized
They were working nights and days!

In only seven days their numbers grew
To more than the dirty oil war soldiers
That in seven months
King George could accrue.

By the day the Queen was to host
"Poetry and the American Voice"
Thousands of poets were speaking out.
THEY FELT THEY HAD NO CHOICE!

They knew they had
important work to do,
that poets have to speak
words that must be spoken.

The day the Queen tried to silence the poets
poets recited poems carefully selected.
Millions world-wide gathered to listen
and War was rejected!

Dedicated to Poets of the world

Watching Birds

Sparkling snow crystals,
reflecting mid morning sun,
decorate thick white blanketing snow
textured with bird claw prints.
The temperature slowly rises
from the night's below zero low.

Rationed egg, three slices of turkey bacon
washed down with strawberry kiwi herbal tea,
I sit spying through kitchen windows
at tufted titmice and diligent wrens
carefully searching under empty feeders
snatching remaining spilled seeds.
Others peck away at suet hanging from gutters
in recycled mesh tangerine bags.

I "blew it," I realize. I did not get in enough bird food
before lingering snowstorms trapped me on this beloved hill.

Trying to forgive myself, I wonder if oatmeal is harmful to birds.
I make plans to call, to question the county agent,
then lay them aside.

I relax.

Enjoying the stress-free morning,
I listen to my music CD
produced especially for me… a gift from my beloved Lolly.
Beautiful love songs get to me… sadden me.

Having no lover can be difficult.
The songs bring tender memories
of a much loved, very romantic dead one.

I try unsuccessfully to accept a thought…
the likeliness I'll never have romance in my life again.
I try to embrace this loss.
You must be careful, a wise wren chirps,
about the kind of music you choose to play.

Snow, pushed by wind, falls dramatically
from high limbs to ground
frightening birds while Moulin Rouge tango music
gets loud, the violins get passionate.

Too bad, I think, no one is here
to share this enjoyment with me.
Maybe he will come someday…
maybe a violinist?
Then, I realize, he is here…for a visit.

Warm song lyrics fill my kitchen.
"If I were a painter and could paint a melody,
I'd climb inside the swirling skies to be with you,
I'd climb inside the skies to be with you."
Birds linger, spying at us through kitchen windows.

We dance the morning away.

Dedicated in memory of Terry Green

CAROL PAIVA

Carol Paiva (born 1948, New Haven CT) arrived in the Midwest on a 747 in January 1971 and, on the descent over Indianapolis, immediately saw from the lay of the land that this wasn't New England. In Bloomington IN, equipped with a B.A. in English Lit, she luckily found part-time work (though on a two-week trial basis) assisting a bookbinder and has been in the bindery ever since, except for two years' study for a Master of Fine Arts in painting at the University of Notre Dame ('74).

Painting, poetry, cats, and cooking are among the things dear to her heart, as well as conversation, corduroy, silk, silver, stories, pampas grass, chicory blooms, peonies, hollyhocks, Virginia creeper, coffee, woolens, and assorted items loosely termed tchotchkes. A few poets on her list of favorites are Elizabeth Bishop, Federico Garcia Lorca, Gerard Manley Hopkins, Wallace Stevens, and Wisława Szymborska.

Braking for Hummingbirds

For Kathleen Anderson

My friend's feeder with its satellite ring
perches above red impatiens
below the sill of the high, screened window over the sink;
calls in wee sippers
wide of observation, quick in perspicacity
and well-versed as a pirate's good eye. Then,

flitter, flutter, whirr, wings
ripple swift as water. Aye,

sunlight in the yard behind them,
on its golden schedule,
makes it seem
miraculous, silhouettes brief as these
should carry this momentous depth of vivacity
and sail distinctively on common air:

they drink, drink
black needle-nose
to the nectar. Dip Dip Dip
unlike prose.
Poke again and away they go, winks on wing,
solo, a jewel of metaphor.
Each tippling a facet of the art;
sipping the heartbeat.

Saturday Morning Coffee

Monocle: eye of the clock
across the room catches
rebounded window light, casts
a cloud-bright stare on me
deep in my companion chair;
a mug half-full of coffee
beside me, steaming the air
with its breath. Saturday coffee

bides its own tick and time,
and together we slip
down a narrow, billowy stair,
into a steamy, delicious chase,
aweigh down fathoms

rife with half-light flora and fauna
from last night's dreams

while painted dogs with painted eyes,
in place on the shelf,
companionably guard the Cyclopean clock
and measure time in clay.

The Namaycush*

Shaky with heat lasting two weeks, too
long, into October

we want to search for namaycush
in deep cool lakes
anywhere from Maine to Vancouver.

A stout trout with a light belly
swims in our minds,
spawns dreams in flesh,

dreams descrying us in wool, then
winter with dripping branches
bare and black, like old leather.

Awhile we paddle up leafy rivers,
drink from tepid cups, man the oars
not far from shore, careful
to watch for shoals.

For now is the season
of dark cottons.

*Namaycush, according to Webster, is derived from the Cree and is a large,
speckled trout of the lakes of North America from New England to Alaska.

The Eternal City

In the circle of seven hills, before papal pomp,
before any declension of the seven deadly sins:

Triumphs of the Caesars arranged the marbles and travertine
along the Tiber, turned sun-strewn thoroughfares
into blazing chains of glory blare.

Grey quadrupeds mountainous in years, in size
stepping heavily on hewn stone.

Roaring cats full-muscled, fierce
with bracelets at paws, gaudy and
sleek in patterned coats,
give opulent voice to shackles straining their throats.

The Queen of all Egypt arrayed
in rivers of sun-flamed gold, with black eyes.

Raptors whose javelin sight
bides the cold-blooded slide of day, hooded
auguries of fin, fur and feather
enthralled in miles of gut, in steam
and aerie sighs.

Booty of steel, speared enterprise,
breastplates of bone, mineral finds,
flacons royal in form and foreign wine
building cages for the circus of the mind.

On the hoof, horns' span
exceeding the height of a man, the bull
bronzed in hide; his cabochon eyes — when plucked
from their sockets and prepared for the table —
please the guests at grace, at pleasure,
on coveys of cushions while peacocks' serenades,
sweet as the play of *putti*, brighten polished laughter
and punctuate the flow of classic conjuration.

Feasting. Lamps. Breeze of lyres
while servers' shadows lengthen on the walls.

Tines

You wash dishes every day,
clean the tines, to shine, to hold
no debris of missed morsel.
Every day at the sudsy sink;
a bite of spring, its tide
of mild water; the swirl,
the fresh downpour from the spout.

You swish cleansing liquors
over the plates, both sides,
be sure the glasses are bright
and clear. And in the spring

in this hemisphere, mad March
or thereabouts, you find
your belly hungry after each meal.

Therefore,
you know one reason, at least
some poets linger
like animals on all fours,
held in the teeth of an open window.

At Beatrice Wells's, West Haven

Grey shingles on the veranda. House cat grey,
its edge of crispness like a summer day without sun at the ocean.
The broad front walk, fine and so slightly inclined,
overlooked the town green, trees old and tall,
painted benches with scrolling iron legs
near narrow paths of creamy cement, complementing Mrs. Wells's
front door,
a honey of varnished oak, set with a gem of beveled glass
whose plain brilliance

and karat weight swept through the foyer
where the girls would peel their coats and jackets
down to stripling leotards of plain black,
ready to don their slippers
and cross the polished hardwood floor
to her wide-open living room, a flood of window-shine,
and line up before the mouth of the massive fireplace
for lessons. Mrs. Wells's color was solid

Copenhagen blue; bunting of the bluest
smock which reached the magnitudes of her calves.
Its pleated wing of swaying form never could
upstage the firm magnificence of flame, the upsweep she wore.
With fully fuschia lips she sang succinct, sweet commands
through the essential steps of the dance positions
which her assistants, tall, trim, and bent to perfection,
demonstrated with their pearl earrings like fresh catches from the sea.
And the beginners strove over the steps;
the grappling, the thriving, the naturally adept.

Upon the shore of the dance, unseen,
a little girl wept to be tall,
entranced with waves in harmony
licking, licking the beaches along Savin Rock, sandy paws,
grains and pebbles, houses of hermit crabs.

Wide-eyed, wordless with recall
the little girl tip-toed on hot sand, to explore
the multicolor mound of flesh,
a Portuguese man-of-war someone had dared
to fish up with a deep wire basket
that sunners and swimmers came to stare at
near the long, greyed pier.

Pliés moving, in imitation of waves,
of scaly silence. And she wept.
Drab had dribbled in.

CAROLYN GRIFFIN

Carolyn Griffin was born in 1967. She learned to read at two and a half and has loved the written word since. She has lived with scoliosis and a variety of health problems.

A lot of her writing helps in dealing with emotions and pain either through humor or the darker genres. She has published two books of short stories and poetry: The Great Release (out of print) and Sidesplittin', Butt Kickin', Tear Droppin' Times under the name C. Griffin via amazon.com.

She joined Wrapscallions in 1999 and has learned a great many things from other writers and readers. She is currently working on a novel and a short story collection. She paints zentangles on clothing, journals, etc. She draws, paints, crafts, and sells these works on request. She loves to learn new forms of expression.

When she's not creating she's enjoying her family, farm and her furry children.

Ian, the Ambulance Driver

A character sketch

The first morning after we moved to the small town I woke to my window opening I sat bolt upright in bed my heart in my throat. Two denim legs climbed in my bedroom. I recognized the man as Ian Richards.

"Oh, where's your brother," he asked?

"His room is on the back of the house." I said, shaking.

"Thanks," he said and walked through my room and out my door.

The next time I saw Ian I almost didn't recognize him. He was in the deli with his wife. He wore a pink dress, violet lip color and pink pumps. I thought it was two women until he turned to say "Hello." I stepped back tying not to show how shocked I was at his attire but I believe he sensed it. Then I tried not to laugh.

"It's his hobby," his wife said. "Hi, I'm Marissa Richards, Ian's wife."

I shook her hand, then watched with amusement as Ian walked casually behind the deli counter and made his own sandwich. It consisted of peanuts, pork rinds, broccoli stems, cashews and cream cheese. He squished this between two slices of bread, then smothered all in a volcano of mayonnaise and mixed grape Kool-Aid with Pepsi.

Marissa said, "He's the only one they'll let make his own."

I mumbled, "To avoid making themselves ill, I bet."

"What?" Marissa asked. Then, without a word from me she said, "Gross appetite huh?"

I nodded. For the first few months Ian helped my brother get his garage business off the ground. If customers took their time returning Ian would call them and threaten to remove items from their vehicles or yard. If that didn't work, he used pure blackmail. This never failed to get customers to return in a hurry.

Ian lost his grandfather due to the distance of towns. The paramedics had to come from thirteen miles away, only to pick up the ailing patient in our town then drive another fifteen to the hospital. After the loss of his grandfather, Ian took matters into his own hands. He began driving folks to the hospital. He would strap the patient into the bed of his S-10 pickup and lie them down on a mattress. It was held in by a bungee cord. He could get to that fifteen mile hospital distance from our town in seven minutes flat, hopefully without the patient floating or flopping about too much on these back roads. After about a year and half of this, the hospital gave Ian his own EMS License and ambulance. Even the oddest folks can have humongous hearts.

Coming To Terms

I used to wonder a whole lot about all the crap
    I ain't got.
I used to cuss my empty drawers
    for being poor as my dull floors.
No money at all in my pockets,
    no cool stuff plugged in my sockets.
Without a good vehicle to drive—
    oh how will I survive.
To be rich would be nice,
    but someone might put me on ice.
They'd steal all I had;
    then I would feel, oh so bad—
They'd even take my bucket.
    So one day I just said, "F__k it."

If It Had Been A Snake, It Would Have Bit You

Lionel Rosenfell and Ella Well Rose were sitting on a bench one summer afternoon. Ella was engrossed in the erotic adventures of someone's antique diaries she had purchased that morning. She had so longed for a tall, slender dandy with dark wavy hair and long erotic fingers. She wanted to be rescued from utter loneliness.

Lionel was flipping through the pages of *Ivanhoe* for the fourth time in his thirty-eight years. He often dreamt of saving a gorgeous damsel with long, blonde hair. Oh how he wanted a quivering classic styled Guinevere to save. He would fight tigers for a girl like that. He wanted her to have her own mind. But she must be slightly shy and humble, not too proud or strong.

Ella dropped her bag of mixed nuts on the bench between them. Lionel heard them fall and politely said, "Here miss, I'm sorry to bother you. But you dropped your snack."

His lengthy fingers scooped up the bag so no more would spill out.

"Thank you kind sir." Ella nodded in humility, then nearly yanked them from his hands never touching him. Still her yank felt more like an airy breeze to Lionel.

Lionel read the rest of his book and dreamt of a weakened maid who needed him. Ella continued with her antique erotic diaries about a woman and her blue-eyed fireman with the long fingers. "

Oh to be rescued and loved like that," she thought.

Suddenly a man came up and grabbed Ella's purse. She screamed as the man knocked her to the ground. Lionel leapt to his feet and pounced on the man, nearly ripping the thief's arm off. He retrieved the purse and took it back to Ella when the man got away and ran off. Lionel knelt on one knee and helped Ella to her feet with one strong sweeping arm and asked, "Are you hurt my lady?"

Ella snatched back her purse, dusted herself off lightly, and said very shyly, "No. I'm fine. Are you okay? Ella let go of Lionel's long slender fingers.

"Yeah, I may have strained a bit to yank your purse away, but I got it back for you." He whispered like a soft breeze in her pinned up golden hair. His legs were apart like a cowboy who rides too long.

"Thank you so much." Ella clutched her purse to her chest and again said, "Thank you for your kindness."

Lionel's deep blue bedroom-eyes stared at a mild scrape on Ella's hand. He took out his clean handkerchief and said, "With your permission, miss?" Then he held it on the bloody scrape, semi-caressing her hand. Then their phones rang.

"Keep that there until the bleeding stops, then discard it," he said.

Each excused themselves and answered their cell phone. On Lionel's phone his girlfriend, a major executive in some export company, was barking orders of where to meet her Friday night. She made plans for them to go bronco busting at some rodeo bar. He hated bulls, cows, and noisy bars, but agreed to go. No one dared argue with the executive. Still he longed for her just once to ask him what he wanted to do. But her blonde, short hair was a semi-turn-on. Not quite the long wavy hair of King Arthur's Guinevere. But a close shorter version. Too bad she never wanted to stay home long enough to have a few hours together while he played with that blonde crop she called hair.

Ella was talking to her boyfriend Spike. He had just finished practicing with his punk band "Bedroom Brawlers" and wanted her to drop by on her way so they could get matching piercings and maybe a tattoo. Ella reluctantly agreed, although Spike wasn't the type to demand a thing from her. Still she loved him didn't she? He did have strong drummer's hands, but with stubby fingers. He did let her "run off leash" as Spike put it. Sometimes a bit too carelessly. To the point of ignoring one like that purse snatcher today.

She turned to face Lionel, her hair slowly slipping from it's pinned up contraption. "Thank you again, for saving my purse." Ella smiled shyly.

Lionel waved his long fingers at her and continued saying, "Yes dear, I know dear," into his phone.

He walked away west and Ella east. As she walked, she yanked the hair from her bun and let it fall so softly over her puffy sleeved jacket, cascading it to the top of her long green skirt. She glanced back once to meet eyes with the long slender purse-hero who waved again. He flashed his deep serious blue eyes at her.

"Nice man," she thought. But surely not her erotic hero like the ones she loved to read about in old novels and diaries. She continued on trying to build up the courage to get the piercings and tattoos Spike wanted them to get together.

Lionel went home to search dating sites out of curiosity for a long-haired classic beauty who just wanted to stay home some nights and play together.

Beyond The Corn

I am envious of all who've been beyond the corn to the
    mountains and oceans.

Poor to the bone and sheltered, stuck in the center of
    the midwest.

Dad's ideal vacation was the state park. But he has long passed.

I have the freedom, but not enough cash to go beyond the corn.

But I have been to me. Dark secrets of a stoner's nights
    surviving it and sobering up due to death's threatening gaze.

Inner madness of weekly nightmares take me on a journey
    of soul.

Drowning in pain since birth, I am the captive of bad health.

I've not been beyond the corn. But pain makes creativity
    flourish to the depths of a bitter heart created by harsh
    violent ex-lovers and a few crude and dishonest friends.

I've not been beyond the corn, but I've been to me.

Beyond the corn, to the mountains and oceans.

Romantic Gift Suggestions From a Hill-Jack Male

Forget chocolate, after all you want your woman to keep that Hollywood beach figure you two always wish she had, right? You could try flowers, but why, they grow around here like grass. Both types of grass — smoking and non. As a hill-jack man, you are boss and in charge of your woman. So get her somethin' different. Always get her something you can enjoy too. Start off with something special just for her. Go to the Super-center Store and buy some girls' soap or shampoo.

Make sure there ain't no picture of dogs or cats on the label though. While she likes pictures of fuzzy critters, their shampoo is bad for her hair. Only buy her ladies' shampoo on two conditions; one, she has indoor plumbing with clear water or straight mud. No chemicals. Two, make sure she knows how to use such luxuries as shampoo or can at least read directions.

If not, you yourself could learn how to use them and then teach her. Or better yet, take a class on it together. Maybell Sanders down at the groomers taught me and my girl. Blindfold your woman so she doesn't see Maybell's sign out front. Trust me, it makes her mad.

If this doesn't sound like something you care to get your woman, or if she's the learned type with her own bottles of shampoo, try engraving your name on a large two-by-two rock and tying it to her ankle. This is a traditional romantic gift from way back. Even if someone else has to help you spell your name out. Trust me, there's no other legal way to tell the world, "This is my woman!" If your woman accessorizes a lot, try making her a purse with fishing line and feed bag.

Make certain the type of livestock animal the feedbag is for shows on the outside of the bag right under her name which you can have someone, say her pretty sister, sew on for you. Have the sister visit to sew when your woman ain't home. That way, if you ever tire of your girl, you already know the sister from those sewing visits so you can start to date her.

It doesn't take much to make feed bags into classy dresses either. Just have your woman's pretty sister sew it with fishing line and add a cow bell for an accessory. Think of how special she'll feel as she walks down the street the bell tinkling her presence. All the attention she'll get will fill her with joy.

If your woman doesn't like the words "for sows only" on her feed bag dress, you can always use fabric paint and put your name between for and only. That way, every man she meets will know who she belongs to. To make her feel beautiful, add a drawstring belt around the waist. Even if she can't get it completely around her.

Or what if your woman is thin and hot? Take a cue from that pop-diva of the eighties and glue two metal engine funnels together. This makes very sexy lingerie stuff. Have her wear it on all trips, that way it can be used if you break down on the road. As for her underpants, have her sister sew some corn husks together. Or better yet, tell her "I like it showing honey." That way, she won't long for panties.

If all else fails, get wrestling tickets — at least you'll have a great night. Or buy yourself a case of beer and tell her it's a symbol of your love. This way she doesn't have to buy it tonight for you and she can save her money for a case for you some other night. She'll appreciate not having to drive down to the store for the case. Now that's love.

Whatever you get her, don't forget to tell her these romantic words, "Honey, the moon rises and sets with you, especially on our furniture." Take it from another hill-jack man, she'll love you for it, or else.

Who Has the Sign?

There is panic in the street of the small town. The new sign on the edge of town has been stolen. Who or what could commit such a crime is the talk of the town. A few days ago they posted a sign of reward to the person who has information on who took the sign. The reward is only ten dollars however, so no one is bothering to come forward with any suspects. Some even commented, "Who misses the sign anyway? All the thing said was "Welcome to the town of the 1953 basketball champs."

Nothing much is left in the town. All of the stores have moved out. Only one garage, a post office and a fish hatchery are left. Women still wear the Dolly Parton hair-dos. Children still play stick ball in the afternoons.

Two weeks have gone by without any word about the sign. So the three members of the town council gathered in old Mason's pasture and decided to commission ole man Roy to paint the next sign.

Roy never cared for the town. It was just another needle in Earths' burning hay stack. So the signs he painted as testers are not exactly what the town wants. Such signs as: *Welcome to Hillbilly Hell; Quick! Turn back before they get you; The grass is greener here, so dry your own; Welcome to granny's dirty elbow* and the favorite of several opposing townsfolk, *Welcome, we make Deliverance look like Mayberry.*

The town is quite old-fashioned, but not as bad as Roy makes it out to be. The town council went into a panic knowing there soon be summer tourists driving through looking for small towns such as this to start a small business and have a quiet residence. So, they warned Roy, if he doesn't have a good sign worthy of the town's greatness in two weeks, they will withhold payment and commission another painter.

So with great reluctance, Roy said he'd make a sign that reads, *Welcome to the little town that grew overnight.* "It's acceptable," said the town council. But none heard Roy when he walked away muttering in a quiet grumble, "When hell freezes over." By mid-summer the three men of the town council watched tourists drive right past real estate signs and leasing signs.

Roy began a new business of painting signs on the side of barns and sheds while the owners were away. He remained anonymous but his art work and text caught plenty of attention from everyone, including some disgruntled town council members and some humiliated property owners.

Daddy's Dutiful Daughter

All I know about tomorrow
　　is it will be worse than today.
You taught me that
　　in all sorts of philosophies you created.
I only sacrificed my future
　　to make certain you'd be fine.
I walked on eggshells
　　all the friggin' time, even now.
You always treated me|
　　like I was committing a crime.
When I would leave the house for an hour
　　I, your prisoner.
What I could have been,
　　if I'd just been myself, not yours.
I gave up all I was
　　to make sure life was easy on you.

PETE SEBERT

Storyteller, poet, minister, schooled in Indiana, Tennessee, Kentucky and by more than colleges, guided by grandmas, grandfathers, little ones and others, blood kin and more. I watched and listened to them along the way, soaked up the poems, stories and paintings wherever in Logansport, Berea, Tipton, Knoxville, Indy and Lexington. Then to Brown County where these hills have ears, plus the eyes of the people, visitors and natives must accept the blame for my telling and re-telling if there is such a thing for blame. Because without all of you listening and smiling and telling your tales I would not have developed this ability to tell what I see and hear.

Von

When it came his turn to sit at the head of the table with
his bride and four offspring, he wore them out with his
daily life lectures in the university of Brown County
College of Truths, Half Truths and Outright lies

After bride died and the children scattered,
He needed listening ears and admiring eyes,
as we all do to maintain our curiosity and creativity
to make the effort to keep it on

So he opened wider the door to his kitchen and started
Wrapscallions "Writers, Readers, and Poets Society."

It was his going out to meet other sojourners on the
dry and dusty road and often damp wet trail,
inviting us to sit together around a table.
Afterward it was off to the Pine Room.
Later when his energy was down and the oxygen low
to his watering and gathering hole we would go

No dollars needed to enter, you only had to bring
an ear plus a story or two and some time sitting on the
deck of time. Taking time to sit with the founding
father of the Wrapscallions.

His home especially his kitchen became a
community watering hole
Brown Country storytellers met there a few times.
Where when ever the urge and need for laughter,
stories and reassurance came upon you, you could go to Von's.

A Storyteller is Born

On 5th Street in Dayton, Ohio from 1943-1946 I would crawl up on my grandfather Karn's lap. I still feel his chest rumble as he laughed, it rippled through him and made me happy and secure during WWII while my father was away. As I grew, this habit of getting close to the action put me in the front row in class, in church or in a group to be part of what was occurring. The desire was not to lead but be part of and not miss anything. Today it is to encourage and share wherever I am. It happens to me today as I am in a group I lock my eyes on the speaker because I am hungry to know and be part of something alive. They return the favor by looking at me and helping me fill my mind and heart with the best they have.

Along the Wabash River near Logansport from 1947 to 1954 my parents would read to me or I would read the Bible stories and sing choruses of overcoming the giant or the small child growing up. As a fourth grader in Cass County, I won the award for reading over 100 books during a library summer reading program most of the time under a large shady bush, laying on my stomach.

For a time in high school I sometimes too often made the funny remark to call attention to myself or took the short cut to get the laugh. Through the years I studied the spoken word and observed speakers or by myself read until I fell asleep with a book on my chest and it would wake me up several hours later as it fell on the floor. In past ten years the books or cds were of Brown County people and history. Sometimes I would pick it up and read until finished or I feel asleep again.

When Stephani and Shon, my daughter and son, now in their 40s were children, I gave them gifts of tickets they could give to me and I would do what the ticket said, some of those were stories about them when they were little or of their mother and dad when we were young.

When I came to Brown County in the spring of 1997 to manage the Orchard Hill Inn as a bed and breakfast, I began to read the artists and pioneer stories while listening to Slats Klug's and Steve Miller's, *Liars Bench,* then when *My Brown County Home* came out with Slats and the series of CD that followed I listened to them over and over. Because they tickled me, inspired me and put words on my thoughts. When people ask me what is the best way to get Brown County history ever since I've recommended the first two CD's as capturing the spirit, ornyness, wonder and fun of Brown County.

But the best storyteller is still Abe Martin, in a sentence or in the almanacks Kin Hubbard walks away with that prize. He puts a story in so few words you won't forget it or you don't need a dictionary or teacher to tell you what it means. David Yaseen, a dear friend, for whom I worked for the last two years of his life, planned to become a story teller at Abe Martin Lodge. He and Andy Rogers had planned this project if David could get his health back enough to get back in his wheel chair. We studied together in 1999 and 2000 read some of the Almanacks. Reading those I began to see how Hubbard used humor to portray his love of life, the questions he had and the respect for ordinariness and contrariness of us all.

Just a year or so before meeting David I heard the first cry of my first granddaughter Sara Ann Stelmach over the phone. How could I tell her of the wonder and the craziness of this world without turning her off? Trained as a preacher and teacher too often my method or a message most valuable was overlooked or ignored by the broader culture or the people who paid me to serve them. How do you remain a person of integrity and still reach out in such a way as will get at least an ear? The lover always learns the language of the loved, is the answer that that key question.

I began to see how the various layers of stories of pioneers, artists, conservations and Abe Martin came together and created the Artist Colony of the Midwest and entered into the myths and minds of America, especially the Midwest. How these stories so common to every village and town, yet were distinctively integrated and created a sanctuary of the spirit and the mind, a place called Brown County. I call it "Brown Country, a place located on the edge of the village forest, in the Hoosier state of mind near the heart of the universe."

All during this time I met with W.R.A.P.S. honing my stories, creating characters and having smiling eyes and friendly ears to develop my courage to move out on the streets and onto the stage. There is no substitute for those Brown County ears and eyes for past 10 years.

What I learned even love about storytelling is it respects us, plays with our minds and makes us think while laughing. When our mouth is spread with a smile or opened with a laugh our mind is open in that instant, an idea is planted by the story, not necessarily by the story teller.

A storyteller is a listener, even though they are known as tellers. First you have listened for years to the tales, tears and thoughts of others; whether they are around a fire, in a book or your own imagination. Roger Bacon wrote, "reading makes a mind full, writing clarifies it." Telling the story earns the ears of listeners and the right to enter someone's memory.

Jacob Brown…an ambassador from another time…emerged while living in these hills as a voice to tell Sara, Faith and Grace, my granddaughters the delights and dangers of life. I'm glad you are listening in, you make me and the values we hold dear more believable to them. I pray, I am the same for you and your little ones.

Schooner Valley Calls

I gave birth to you, surely as you came from your mother's womb
You play in my creeks, hollows and climb the hills & branches from
    my trees.
You lie down at night on my breast, I hear you breathe easily on those
    nights you rest.

I feel the shudder when you shiver from the cold winds of your
    dreams, then awake to see frost on your windows.
I hear your sighs of passion, silent cries for help, the laughter that
    echoes up the hollow.
I watch you grow and seek the sun, along with other creatures and
    green things.

See you gather at Knight's Corner, Belmont Chapel, Mike's dance
    barn, Duncan, the ski lodge that now
Vibrates with gospel singing and the House of the Singing
    Winds, then at evening to your own homes.

Yet so many of you, rush through me on your way to Nashville,
    Columbus or Indianapolis,
Others go west to Bloomington and points beyond especially on
    Hoosier game night or Saturdays to the Opry.
Very few head south, maybe a wandering tourist or a Deckard going
    home.
Those headed North to Yellowwood Lake or looking for a gravesite or
    cemetery remembering the bean dinner.

Oh, how I wish, even pray you'd slow down and look me over, I give
    you so much, with more treasures still in me.
Most of you do for a moment, I see you let off the gas when you see
    me at the top, there by the red barn,
You take a deep breath, sigh at my beauty, then dash down the hill,
    your mind off somewhere else

Not like the Shawnee, Trapper Schoonover or Theodore Clement
    Steele, They stopped, really lived in me,
Long enough to pick and dry berries and venison, trap, skin and cure
    hides, Steele painted my picture often.

Why don't you visit with each other often around the campfire or
    invite each other over for a Sunday evening?
Come sit with me I'll tell you about the Sinns, Hatchetts, Deckards,
    Klinedorfers, Hubers, Robertsons, Wootens Bucholz, Knights,
They still hang around on stones, in memories, books, I knew them
    all well.
But they have already laid down their bones and blood and joined
    forces with me, You still have yours.
Yet you drink my water, breathe my air, eat my minerals, How are
    you doing? I wonder at times about you and your great-great
    grandchildren.

Some of you know me well, you put your hands in my clay, plant
    seeds in me, hunt my game, play in my creeks,
Hollows, climb hills and the branches of my trees, listen to birds
    sing for joy, you even care about the children and great-great
    grandchildren of other people; some of the finest people who ever
    lived in any place, live here.

Who am I, I give birth to you every morning as the sun rises and tuck
    you in at night as it sets.
Some day you will lay your head for the last time on my breast and
    your bones and blood will come back to me.
While your spirit/breath will catch a breeze.

Schooner Valley

Morning's Magic Mist on Goat Hill · © Susan W. Showalter

DEBI HURT

Debi Hurt lives in Scipio, Indiana with her miniature dachshunds. She has a son, a daughter, a step-daughter and five grandchildren.

Debi has been writing since her pre-teen years. She has developed and run several writers groups, offered workshops, seminars and a variety of tools to help up-and-coming and authors hone their craft.

She is the publisher/editor of *Pen It! Magazine,* a bi-monthly magazine for writers which she started in January, 2010, that currently has columnists and subscribers from across the United States: Missouri, Florida, Arizona, and New York.

Debi has several self-published works, including: *The Quest For Shireman* (2010); *Recipes From a Country Cook* (2008); *Ride The Spirit Horse* (2007); *The Daring Adventures of Donnie the Dachshund* (2006); and will soon release *Writing Creatively,* her book on creative writing.

Debi has directed or been involved with several writing organizations: Writers, Readers and Poets Society of Brown County (Nashville, Indiana) since 2006, group leader for 3 years; Events Coordinator

Jackson County Writers Group, director (closed); Bartholomew County Writers Group, director/member since 2008; and the Jennings County Writer's Group, director 2012.

Debi has organized several writer's workshops, three author's fairs in Nashville, Indiana and one writer's conference in Columbus, Indiana. She often is solicited to be a speaker at the Bartholomew County Public Library on self publishing, creative writing, and other subjects.

Debi teaches creative writing at the Mill Race Center in Columbus, Indiana one night per week. These classes are open to the public. You may reach Debi for further information or to purchase any of her books, you may email her at debih7606@frontier.com. She would welcome your questions and feedback. You may visit her website at www.penitpublications.com/penitmagazine.com

Looking For The Summer Sun

"Excuse me," I said to the man with the bun
    "But, I'm looking for the Summer Sun.
      Have you seen it's glowing face around here?
      I've felt it's warmth, so it must be near."

He looked up at me, with ketchup on his mouth and said,
    "Just tell me what this is all about?"

"Well, you see I said, I've misplaced the Sun.
    I'm tired of the Cold and ready for some Fun."

"I see," he said, "but you've asked the wrong man.
    Go, up this road and ask for Stan.
      He's got a little farm and an almanac.
      I'm told Stan can bring that ole Sun back."

So, I headed up the path he'd set me on.
    I got there quickly, it didn't take long.
      Ole Stan was working way out in a field of dead corn.
      Seeing his place made me a little forlorn.

It made me miss home, but I digress.
    So, I asked Ole Stan to tell me, to confess.
      "Has the Sun run away, has she left us for good?
      I'm so tired of wearin' this coat with a hood."

Ole Stan looked up from his plow and said,
    "Are you crazy, young man?" His face was all red
      "It's only March, it's still Winter here.
      The Sun will be back soon, have no fear.

"But, you must give it time to rest and relax.
    So, when she comes back, she can shine at her Max.
      Now, just come inside and we'll eat and we'll Sup.
      We'll have a nice meal, but we won't bring this up.
    "Cause" if you keep lookin' for the Summer Sun,
      You'll spoil her vacation, you'll ruin her Fun.
      She'll be back in time to warm up our lives.
      And, we'll be happier still when she finally arrives."

Mr. Turkey

We regret to inform you that your son, Plump E. Turkey has met with an untimely death. He expired on Thanksgiving Day. The day was a real "scorcher" for him. He started out luxuriating in a milk and butter bath, but the heat of the day overcame him. He finally succumbed after being roasted for about 5 hours. Unfortunately, he could not be revived.

We would, however, like to assure you that he was well loved. Those who knew him intimately indicated that he was quite a tasteful fellow. He always had a golden glow about him. He was a real humanitarian. He was known to have fed many of the hungry in the neighborhood. His best friends, Mash E. Tato and Sage Dressing were by his side when he passed from this world.

Please accept our sincere condolences.

Sincerely,

Mr. Turk E. Farmer

PS: If you have any more children as warm and tasteful as Plump E. Turkey, we would be happy to have them join us next year for our annual Thanksgiving dinner.

Trouble in Farmland!

Mr. Do Berry came strolling in one morning about 4:00 AM after having been out all night. His wife Rasp Berry, met him at the door. "Just where have you Bean?" she asked. "Nice of you to Turnip?" To which Do Berry replied, "Well, Pumpkin, I have been out with my Squash buddies playing a night game." "Really?" replied Ms. Berry, "Then what is that Catsup on your Collard? You have been with that Tomato again haven't you? Don't you Carrot all about me?"

Mr. Do Berry's face turned a little Radish in color. He was Pea -O'd. "Now listen here, woman." He said, "I Artichoke you. I Yam so tired of you accusing me of going with that Ginger. I never touched her. You are, and have always been, the Apple of my eye. No one could ever comPear with you. With that Cherry nose and RoseHips of yours. Orange you ever going to trust me? I would never do anything to hurt you or our kids, little Straw Berry or little Boisen Berry. You three are my life. I am Plum over these accusations."

Well, RaspBerry was taken aback. She was so used to him Garden his feelings. He never opened up like this. With Watercressed eyes she looked at Do Berry and said, "Lettuce try to never fight about this again. I've been Beeting myself up over this when I should have known better. You are a wonderful father and have always been there when it comes to Raisin our kids. And down the road I see you as a fabulous PawPaw. So, my Passionfruit, Lettuce put this behind us. I am truly sorry." And the Berries were never sour in Farmland again!

Who Will Remember Me?

Who will remember me
 When my days are done?
Who will remember me
 When I've had my run?
Who will smile
 When I cross their mind?
Who will be sad
 that I've left them behind?
Will you shed a tear
 because I've gone away?
Will you remember me
 with only good things to say?
If I have made an impression.
 And changed even one life.
 I'll go meet my maker
 with no worries, no strife.
So, remember me
 when I'm no longer here
 and always remember that
 I loved you my dear.

PAUL SHRIVER

Dr Shriver is a semi-retired clinical and forensic psychologist, currently practicing part-time in Bloomington, Indiana. He has worked in this field since 1964, and for 26 years, until 2003, was principle psychologist at the Indiana Women's Prison in Indianapolis. He is married, with three stepdaughters.

He lives at Lake Lemon. Originally from Mattoon, Illinois, and educated at Bradley University in Peoria and Indiana University, he has been a "Hoosier" for 35 years. Shriver has published two volumes of his collected poetry, photos, essays, and songs: *The Girl and the Cat (Singing People with Songs in Them)* and *Earthbound—(translations from the Martian)*. Shriver is a member of Bucks n' Does square dance club, Brown County Dulcimer society, and W.R.A.P.S. (Writers, Readers and Poets Society of Brown County). His poetry has won national and international Awards. *Poor Auntie*, a one-act play, is his first, and is based on an actual incident during one of his vacations many years ago.

A Vote Speaks

I am the key
I am fitting

I turn to the left
The bolt slides free
The door unlocks
Possibility awaits
The open door

I turn to the right
The bolt shoots home
The door locks
Possibility
Sealed within
The closed door

Or I may
Withdraw
Of no more use, then
Am I
Turning not

A difference
Is mine to make
Turn I must

A door opened
A door closed
I begin
It is my turn

I am the key
I am fitting

Caterpillar Negotiates Blacktop

(Thoughts on the BP 2010 Gulf Oil Disaster)

Intelligence
The exclusive province
Of the "big brainers"
So foolish by contrast
The choices of the lowliest
On the rising ladders
Of evolutionary progress

Of simple worms
From the highly evolved
Reasoning of
Educated engineers
Digging deep
Their well-planned wells
Into the unknowable

Halfway
Across the asphalt
However seldom dared
Surely enough
I spied there this
Wooly worm
Committed to his choice

Unsurprised, I
As the sudden cyclist
Unheeding creepy crawlers
Cut short this small career
In retrospect
Bold but foolhardy
Unwise worm

Humping it
Hoping and seemingly
Doggedly determined
To reach the farther side
Its viewpoint
Slightly truncated perhaps
Or perhaps not

And yet,
To such a small and
Fuzzy mind
The choice to be made
Must have seemed
A good idea…
At the time!

Observing
Its steady progress
Despite the obvious
Risk it must have calculated
I mused
As poets sometimes are wont
How different the delusions

Fox Squirrel Lament

The Anti-Squirrel "Masacree" Song · Tune: Blue Skies

When I hike on the trails,
watch for the fox squirrels'
bushy tails
Red squirrels chatter at me
gathering acorns from each tree

Never saw the woods lookin' so
bright!
autumn is here —
everything right!
September days, hurryin' by,
squirrel season comin',
I could just cry!

You red squirrels
Better go hide!
High in your snug nests —
deep inside!
Don't mind buryin' nuts!
Better make scarce your fuzzy
butts!

Cause in October, hunters come
out!
Bangin' away! I want to shout!
Fox squirrels got to hurry!
Flyin' squirrels fly!
Worry and scurry!
I'll tell you why!

Hunters can't find the gray !
Sportsmen love red squirrels
Blow them away!

Fox squirrels, gone with the
breeze!
Hunters like fleas — do as they
please

Never saw the sky lookin' so gray
Leaves off the trees — all blown
away!
All of the red squirrels
will disappear!
I'll just sit here
tears in my beer!

Poor little fox squirrels
scarce as hen's teeth!
Nothin' but gray squirrels on the
heath!
Fox squirrels — all of them gone!
Ratty little gray squirrels
cover my lawn!

Red squirrels
brightened the scene
Puny, scawny gray squirrels
aren't so keen!

Oh, those pretty
red squirrels!
All of them gone!
Nothin' but gray squirrels
From now on !

Poetry

Poetry, if
worth it's salt
must be
something
one may
Memorize
or recite
or sing
or am I just
old fashioned?

Poetry, to
aspire to inspire
should be
something
one would
wish to
read aloud
spellbinding
listeners
every time.

Still, it
mightn't be
        poetry
if listeners say
only : "Just lovely!"
or : "How was
        that
again?"
But it might be
if they say :
        "Hmmmm…"
or, even better:
"OH,
YES !"

The Dead Bolt

Transcriber's note: What follows is taken from what appears to have been a "vacation journal" or diary. It was found at the rear of a top shelf in a closet by a workman who was demolishing one of the last remaining cabins of an abandoned and derelict "resort" on the Southeast side of "Kabetogama," the largest of the many lakes in Voyageurs National Park on the US/Canadian border. Earlier entrees chronicle pleasant woodland hikes, magnificent weather and scenery, cozy cabins, canoe excursions, and good fishing. The following entrees were the last. The rest of the several pages were blank.

Northwoods Vacation

September 10, 2011: We're slightly disconcerted this first afternoon up here in The Voyageur's area as we edge our way past the clutter of tools and fishing poles toward the equally cluttered registration desk of this somewhat decrepit "lodge" to encounter the robust but very solicitous lady owner, her aged mother, the cook, and the raggedy handyman— not quite what the "World Wide Web" indicated we would find as advertised here on our country's far northern border, but certainly as rugged as the general area appears to be.

Our names are taken and we are directed to our cabin and promised a delicious evening meal once we get settled. The dining area does appear somewhat more inviting, and already some delectable intimations waft through the screens on the autumn breezes from the porch grills.

Slightly distracted, I can't help but comment on one incongruity I noticed outside, turning to the "handyman. "What's that big ol' backhoe for? The one down by the docks? Looks ancient! Does she run?"

"Oh, sure, she runs sure enough," he grins. "And she's for diggin'— mostly — dontcha know?"

It's really more of a grimace than a grin — and not particularly pleasant! The gums are red and raw and look sort of infected, and the teeth, the few I can see, appear unusually elongated, even for his age, which is indeterminate and impossible to guess, the face wrinkled and leathery — sun and wind I suppose.

The landlady shoots him a "look" and the "grin," such as it is champs shut!

"You get along now!" (Was that for us or for him?)

"Supper's around about dusk. You don't want to miss it — you already paid for it, you know. Now, be sure not to forget your flashlight! Some of them pathway lights don't work too well!"

So we shuffle outside and drive down to our rustic cabin. The path is rutted, but the cabin, though old, is cute and clean.

9/10 continued: Unpacked — a little while yet to supper. We've come to Voyageur's National Park, hoping for good fishing and a glimpse of the Northern Lights. This so-called "Park" consists almost entirely of water, dotted by islands accessible only by launch or canoe. We are at the edge of the largest "body" in a lengthy "chain." It is beautiful and awe-inspiring, but it's a wilderness out there—vast wild water you can barely see across — nondescript islands shrouded in mist and wolves that howl in the dark — wasn't there a movie like that?

The clouds are gathering now. They seem to press down into the slate waters like slick stones near the edges of riverbeds. The sun set this evening livid and leaden. The restless waves are now bereft of earlier boaters abandoned and there is a plaintive rumbling of distant thunder that seems to be coming from every quarter at once off the echoing hills — even the atmosphere, the very air feels somehow barren. Hardly the sort of place to nurture comfort or relaxation, though the lodge people, odd as they were, certainly seemed accommodating enough…

Vacation journal, 9/10 continued — later: We have been to supper and back now, and at least it was all that they had promised! There were a few things, however in the course of the evening, barely noticed at the time, coming back now to disquiet me… I will be trying to commit some of them to paper this night as the wind outside rises and rises and rises… The "solicitousness" of our hosts continued to be unfailing in its way — as I casually mentioned a few minor concerns from time to time during and after our supper:

"By the way, the light over our stoop seems to be out."

The caretaker chimed right in, "Okey-dokey! We'll get that looked at right away — first thing!"

But it is now quite late and he doesn't seem to be getting around to it. It doesn't matter so much now, as we got back OK, maybe tomorrow.

He did seem to change the subject rather quickly, I thought.

"Say, now!" he mentioned, "Did you know you can see deer right there in your cabin's front yard most any evening? And that's not all!"

"Um hm. Oh, now I think of it — sort of hate to mention it, but there doesn't seem to be an eye for the hook on the front door screen, either!"

He shrugged, "Cain't recollect rightly if there ever was! We're pretty informal around here. You'll enjoy it, though! See all kinds of things out here, ravens and coons — they're ravens, not crows — moose. Of course, got to watch 'em — hard to predict. And that's not all!"

"There was another thing I noticed too, the deck door — the one on the lake side that slides, you know…"

"Oh, sure," he interrupted, slightly testy this time. "That broken latch — I could get ya a broomstick piece for that, but don'tcha see, there's no outside stair. Yer right out there over the water — pretty sunset views and all. Now what could get way up there, I ask ye?"

"Hmmmm. Incidentally, I think you may have forgot to give us a key for our front door lock when we registered."

Now it was the "front desk lady" who answered.

"Oh, now, you see, none of our cabins out here has ever had any keys for the locks at all! Nary a one! Not just yours! Not never since we've had the place! I reckon the former owners seem to have misplaced them — along with who knows what all else! And we've sort of misplaced them too, actually! This place has turned over a lot over the years. Hard to make a go of it ain't it? Way up here and all — but, you know, we just do what we can."

"Yes, now that you mention it, we also noticed that most of the cabins around us seem to be empty!"

"Ain't ye the noticers, though!" cracked the old boy.

"Hush, now, Ben!" she cut him off. "Not to worry yerselfs! It'll be fillin' up this weekend, right enough, you bet!"

Did we say we were worried?

She went on, "You'll soon get used to the quiet. We wouldn't have it any other way! We like it REAL quiet, don't we Ben?"

He chuckled — I didn't care for the sound of it.

"As long as we've been here," she went on, "No one has never come down that road of yours at night — just only our guests!"

Now, we were beginning to worry a little bit, and wonder just why .

This evening, during supper, we did meet apparently the only two other "guests." They were two avid fishermen we secretly dubbed "Geezer and Son." They'd brought in a trophy "Northern" near dusk —nearly 20 pounds — and said after supper they would be heading "out lake" again — this time after walleye. And we were both thinking (we have compared notes) "We're going to be completely alone tonight away up here in a wilderness cabin, and we just met these people. And who the heck are they anyway, really? We're in the North Woods, on the edge of a stormy lake with a "tough gal" landlady, her "sweet old mother," the cook, (a good one, admittedly), and "Old Weird Ben!"

So, right about then was when my wife piped up, to lighten the mood, I supposed. "You know, walking up to the lodge for supper this evening we thought we saw a fox! Ran right across our road! We thought it looked like it had something white in its mouth!"

"Prob'ly jist a rabbit," said the landlady.

But then Ben had to put in his own two bits, as Geezer and Son made their excuses and left for their fishing as the last of the light faded.

"Yup! Get a lot of foxes! Reds, grays, seen babies — kits we calls 'em — all right up around yer place — yep, right there, and not so long ago, neither. And that's not all!" (Pregnant pause)

"Sometimes, ye know, they'll scream in the night — jist on occasion, understand. Sounds sorta like a real baby, er like a child in pain, you know! Don't mind them! It's jist whut they do."

Landlady spoke right up here, somewhat abruptly I thought.

"Pay no mind to Old Ben! He's a good caretaker — none better — but he ain't quite right, you know."

We certainly had began to suspect as much, not that it was any great comfort, but comfort was certainly on the way!

"Now you listen," she said, "If it really matters so much, you got a dead bolt throw, right on the inside of your front door, OK?"

Old Ben seemed to be winding down by this time but he apparently was not quite done. Not quite by a long shot, as it turned out.

"Bears'll walk down yer road, too, sometimes. Sure they do! Saw a "Black Momma" down there couple of days ago! Cubs about sommairs too, I'll wager! And that's not all!"

The Landlady quickly stepped on what seemed to be Ben's favorite phrase.

"We ALL saw her, Ben, wasn't even but a minute, was it? Then she just run off into the woods across from your cabin. They're really quite shy of people, you know, even more so than the wolves, no matter what the papers and magazines would have you believe. So just don't even give it a thought!"

But Ben had one more "bolt" and he chose to "shoot it" right then:

"You know thet pike them two boys got in jist before dinner? By Gar, that was a big un! Oh, I got her all packaged up and she's on ice now!"

This time the lopsided grin was almost a gleeful leer!

"By Gar! Ye know, thet was more like butcherin' a hog than cleanin' a fish!"

This time, her look was downright withering.

"Time you got on right back to your cozy little cabin! High time! And now, hear? You just go on and THROW that big ol' dead bolt lock on that front door pretty soon! You just go on and throw her whenever you want!"

And there didn't really seem to be too much else to say, after that. Out we walked, down that dark road, one small flashlight firmly in hand.

This time the trees seemed to drape and lean from both sides, turning our little path into a sort of claustrophobic, restless tunnel. The wind had died down, but not by much. There was no moon and no stars, and no Northern Lights — just a pallid glow, weaker than our feeble little flashlight, and the silence was palpable. Our way was at first dragging, but ultimately considerably accelerated. In our light's pale glimmer, the formerly colorful autumn leaves were bleached nearly bone-white. Both our steps and time itself seemed like crawling. Then, suddenly far ahead, way too far and much too fast to make out, in the gloom and wavering light — was that merely a shadow, swiftly shifting across the road just beyond our drive? It looked BIG! Or was it merely imagination? Merely my tricky mind toying with my gullible gut? But I wondered, we both did, what's out here with us? What's that big? And that fast? And that can move like that and still make no sound at all? Yet neither of us could speak.

And then — no, it's all right! Never mind! Here's our drive, our cabin door, our dead bolt, our security from things that prowl the night. And within the space of not much more than a breath, we're both inside, safe and now we're laughing at ourselves a bit nervously—almost hysterically, and "What about the lock?" she says, eyes on the bolt.

And so I put a bold face on it, "Oh, not much need of that! The door does latch, even if it doesn't lock! I'm sure that will do the job! After all, we're eating at the lodge and not cooking food in here, just a few snacks. Besides, animals can't open doors like these anyway, even if they wanted to!"

So, that was that! And we had a cup of hot chocolate together and played a game of Scrabble we picked up out of the clutter of the lodge, not all the letters there, but serviceable. And then she went to bed and now she's asleep and I can hear her breathing softly there in the bedroom just off the kitchen area where I sit writing. I think her breathing is the only sound I'm hearing — just that and the wind in the leaves and its whine in the pines, and some branches or something scratching somewhere around the roof.

Well, that's it, then! Our first evening in Voyageur Park! And now it's later — much later, and much darker. Night fell suddenly up here, and solid, like the porticullis of a medievil castle (Spelling? Who cares? Who'll read it but us?)

This silence round about, it feels like waiting. Maybe waiting for the other shoe to drop? It's past midnigghtt, and I'm droozing — getting drosy — nodduning over my journal entrée, here… Ooops!

Entrée? My entrée? Did I really write that just now? Entry! Entry, dammit!

It's been a damn long day! Mentally winding down like the day! Took my pills a while ago — feeling groggy nd loggy 'n froggy—ha ha — ever since that big supper they fed us! Fattening us up, for sure! Just can't get that swift shadow and those words, "Bears walk down here all the time! And that's not all!"

Now what was that supposed to mean? And that last crack, "like butcherin' a daggone hog!" Can't get 'em out of my head —not hardly. So I just got up. I got out of my chair and stumbled over to the cabin door (the roadside door, the unlit door, the forest side door) and I threw that big ol' dead bolt!

That "dead bolt!" And it's off center! It misses the latch catches by a good inch — no way to even put pressure on it to force it!

The rain is beginning to patter and the wind rise again, and now, here in the silence of this darkened room, I can hear the cabin timbers creak and moan, and I wonder, "Is that all?"

The lady and the caretaker, did they smirk as we left to walk that lonely, dark path? To this remote cabin, where not one single door, or screen, or window will latch or lock?

The name, "Sawney Bean" begins to trot a little circle around and around in my head! I'm thinking, "carkers!" Thinking, "things that bite!"

"You rest in peace! — tonight," the lady said.

Could I have heard that right? Is that really what I remember? Not "you have a peaceful rest?"

Damn! Which was it?

What the hell was I thinking — a couple of nimrods coming to a place like this for a "vacation?"

Damn that caretaker and damn that dead bolt!

"You rest in peace!"

Oh, right, not now, damnit! Not this night! No way!

"I'll be damned if I will!"

Northwoods Vacation

September 11, 2011 (9/11 coincidence?) Back from breakfast: eggs, sausage, oj, toast, coffee.

Old Ben is down by the water, putting stuff in a canoe for us. I can see him out the back window. Wife slept pretty good — I'm still "draggin' butt."

Back there after breakfast in the dining room, still bleary-eyed, and there's Old Ben just waiting, it seems.

"Howdja sleep?" he grins that happy face grin.

We tell them about the dead bolt.

"You sure? Oh, well, it looks like it's gonna be a purty day, though you never can tell around here, you know! You gonna take out the canoe, aintcha? Gonna be perty busy around here, I 'spect, but that bolt, sure, I'll get to her first chainst I gets!"

"You jist enjoy yer paddle round th' lake and don't fret it! Be back by suppertime, sure! Sumpin' SPECIAL on th' menu!"

Ben leers, flicks something off his mustache with a VERY long tongue.

OH, GOD! TWO MORE NIGHTS TO GO!

Deer on Goat Hill · © Susan W. Showalter

DEBORAH BOWDEN

Mary Deborah Bowden first developed a love of story-telling and writing from her father, Bradley Garrison Patrick, when she was very young and began creating her own tales in the 1970s. She taught English and creative writing in the public schools and college for 25 years.

She is the author of five books: *Dandelions and other Weeds: A Collection of Musings, Memories, Songs, Poems, and Stories; The Sack Lunch,* illustrated by her talented daughter; *The Adventures of Mister Bramble Bones,* a series about a happy skeleton and his cat Grim; *Felicia Tales: The Many Misadventures of Felicia Brown,* grown from the stories her father told; and *Pat and Little Pat: A Slightly Unconventional Cookbook from a Dad and Daughter.*

In the works are *Daylilies and Nightshades,* a sequel to her *Dandelions* book; *The Adventures of Mister Bramble Bones and Grim,* second in the series; and *The Lestoil Dolls: Promotional Dolls from the Late 1950s.* Ms. Bowden has contributed articles and stories to *The Reflection Rag,* a quarterly publication, *Pen-It Magazine* for writers; and *The Realm,* an on-line magazine of the paranormal. Her writings have appeared in *Kairos: 1970; Midwest Poets from Pen to Paper, Treasured Moments,* an anthology; and *The Wishing Well: Discoveries. Folksy Tales and Remedies* will soon appear in the on-line magazine, *Kentucky Mountain Living.*

Her books can be found at the Book Loft in Nashville, Indiana. The Sack Lunch and *Dandelions and Other Weeds* are on Amazon.com and Barnes and Noble by order, and eBooks-Online.com.

Black, White, and Gray

Blessed are the ignorant
For they shall sleep at night.
To them, the world and all they see
Is cast in black and white.
It is the old and hoary heads
That see the shades of gray.
This steals from them their worthy sleep
Until the break of day.

A Fairy Wedding

Serenades from insects in tree heights,
Strings of fireflies cascading soft lights,
There'll be a fay wedding soon tonight.

All through the day small hummingbirds flit,
This way and that, invitations sent.
A starlit sky, the sun is spent.

Down in the woods, a fay circle glows,
Made of white mushrooms; quickly it grows.
It's proud purpose, a sacred enclose.

Outside the circle, covering the ground,
Pearly shell platters with foods abound;
Silver cups of wine for toasts are found.

The gentle low breezes ruffle the air,
Wafting perfumes of the night flowers fair;
Nicotina's a favorite, all are aware.

Guests are arriving by two's or by one;
Faces are smiling, ready for fun
When vows are said and ritual done.

Small owls in white suits usher them in;
Rabbits, raccoons, and even a wren
Mix with fay folk, anxious to begin.

Rev. Brown Sparrow nods to the choir.
Night birds start singing, insects up higher.
Comes the best man, playing his lyre.

The groom's men follow, voices in song,
All in harmony, no note is wrong.
Then sudden silence; now sounds a gong.

Pixies above drop silvery dust.
The maid of honor in dress of rust
Leads the ladies, similarly trussed.

All now are waiting, facing the aisle,
Down walks the groom, solemn all the while,
Ring bearer, flower girl wave and smile.

The blushing bride's a beautiful sight
 Beaded, shimmery, silvery white,
Long flowing veil behind her so bright.

Bride and groom together, hands interlace,
The Celtic goddess will grant them grace.
By two rings joined, a pledge face to face.

Light the marriage candle, man and wife.
Strike up the band; play bagpipes and fife.
They are one through happiness and strife.

Up they fly now in the night air.
Fairies and pixies all join them there.
Magic dust, fire lights, a sight most rare.

Silver cups with wine are passed to all.
Loud toasts spoke round, shake the forest wall.
Laughter, merriment, so grand the ball.

Let the songs began; dance, feast and drinks.
An owl circles left, holding two minks.
Revelries won't end 'til the moon sinks.

Wedding cakes are cut and passed around,
Then all is eaten except one's crown.
The bride and groom stand upon its mound.

Bells are ringing; folks shout to the pair,
"May your lives be long; your children fair."
Next, bawdy jokes started by the hare.

Ah, the food is gone; the wine is spent;
A pixie sleeps, o'r his plate is bent.
The guests are yawning; it's time they went.

Now in the forest a silence grows.
The fireflies' light just barely glows.
A fairy wedding is at its close.

The Rocker

The little rocker with a caned seat had belonged to her great grandmother, Agnes Carson. The fact that it had no arms made it perfect for Great Grandma to rock her infant son over many a happy hour. When Grandpa David became a young boy, he delighted in holding onto the seat and rocking back and forth as fast as he could. It became his horse Tom-tom, and many were the cowboy battles they won together. As he grew old, he needed a bigger rocker with sturdy arms to help him get up and down. He gave Tom-tom to his daughter Belle.

She had the light oak refinished and buffed to a high sheen and found an expert caner to duplicate the pattern of the worn-out seat. She proudly kept her restored heirloom in the bedroom and allowed no one, not even herself, to sit on it. Sometimes her own daughter Angela would slip into the room when Belle was gone and gently sit on the forbidden seat. Then she too would begin to rock faster and faster until Tom-tom rode the wind. She became a Bedouin princess sailing her carpet across the Egyptian desert to a hidden oasis and cave filled with jewels and magical objects. Sometimes she would forget the real world around her as she rode. Then her mother would catch her in the rocker and give her a lecture on its age and history. She wouldn't punish her, however, because she remembered the Tom-tom tales her father had told her.

In time, Belle moved the rocker into the family room and allowed her daughter full reign over Tom-tom. She realized the little antique needed to be loved and used, not hidden away. When Belle died, the rocker came to live with Angela. She too gently cared for it, but her own daughter Fay was too old to enjoy it, and it held no magical attraction for her. So when Angela needed money to pay her cancer bills, Tom-tom and many other valuables were sold. Before it left the family in the back of an antique seller's truck, she penciled "Tom-tom" and the family names on the bottom of its seat, then sealed it with urethane. Angela cried when her old friend left.

A year later in another town, the little oak rocker with its spindled and knobbed back sat in an antique store's display window. It caught the eye of a pretty pregnant brunette. She walked past the window every Saturday for several weeks. She just knew that rocker would be perfect for rocking her newborn-to-be to sleep. Finally she had saved up the money to buy it and resolved that today was the day.

She didn't haggle over the price with the dealer, and he agreed to have his son deliver it to her apartment at six o'clock that evening. She paced all afternoon. It seemed an eternity until her rocker arrived and was carried upstairs to the baby's awaiting bedroom. Eagerly she tipped the young man and sent him on his way. Then she sat down on the caned seat, pushed back, and released her knees. It moved forward with a silky motion. She smiled.

She rocked in it often over her last trimester. It helped ease her back from the baby's weight. When her son Dan was born, she enjoyed rocking him over the hours. As he grew old enough to sit in the little rocker, he named it "Horsey," and they thundered over the western plains racing the wind.

After he grew up and married, she gave Horsey to him for his pregnant wife. She hoped her grandchild and daughter-in-law would feel the same gentle, comforting motion she had felt during her pregnancy and mothering years. And, she hoped Horsey would still have many long rides left.

However, Anne didn't like antiques and resented having the old thing in her house. Dan tried to get her to sit on it; he knew she would love it when she did. He said there was just something magical about the way it rocked. She refused. She wanted an overstuffed, rocking chaise lounge. She bought one in gray, and relegated the old rocker, over her husband's protests, to the front porch for not-so-welcomed guests to use.

It endured the wind and rain, cold and heat for three years. Its luster was now gone and its caned seat had a crack or two. Still Dan would sit outside many evenings and rock.

In time, Frank, an acquaintance of Dan's from work, began stopping over regularly. He always sat in the little rocker even when offered a large cushioned lawn chair. Sometimes Dan even felt a little jealous of another person sitting on Horsey.

Frank confided that Horsey reminded him of his Grandmother Angela's old rocker Tom-tom. She had rocked him in it when he was a toddler, but had had to sell it. He still had a picture of himself sitting on it back in a family album.

Dan told him that Anne never liked the rocker and wanted to get rid of it. Then both men laughed over women's likes and dislikes, and changed the subject to car racing and basketball.

Two weeks later, Frank returned and spoke to Anne. He begged her to sell the old rocker to him, and after a short pretense of not wanting to sell a beloved, family heirloom, she allowed herself to be persuaded to let it go for $50. The excited man quickly transferred the rocker to his car's back seat before she could change your mind, and making his getaway, took his treasure home. His wife Julia met him at the car when he pulled into the driveway. Proudly he revealed the perfect little rocker to her.

She smiled gleefully and exclaimed, "It's perfect for the family room. I can rock little Mark to sleep on it, and read Janet's bedtime stories while she sits on my lap. The caned seat is still good and will be comfortable."

Frank helped her carry it inside and up the stairs. As he did so, he noticed some penciled words on the seat's bottom. He saw the family names and the word "Tom-tom." Tears filled his eyes as his puzzled wife read the words. She smiled and touched his shoulder.

"Welcome home, Tom-tom," she said.

Vampires

My daughter asked, "Are vampires fact,
and will they come into a flat
through unlatched panes and unclosed doors,
Or search for those outside at play
in darkened light near end of day?"

"Such surely are, oh yes, my dear,
but those which cause all folks to fear
or make them quake within their beds,
are not the souls on movies' screen
and aren't the ones who make us scream.

"Into our chambers these will creep,
on silent wings and tip-toed feet,
and while we think that all is safe,
they steal among us in the night
to pierce our flesh, to suck and bite.

"Elvira plies hypnotic charms
while Varnie grasps with steely arms.
Such cunning tales until we meet:
Mosquitoes, bedbugs, fleas, and lice,
with gnats and chiggers, flies and mites."

The Ice House

Ice is something very common. Whenever a person wants it, the refrigerator is close by. But when I was little, not everyone had an electric refrigerator to make ice. Some folks had big chunks of the cold stuff brought to their house in a truck. Then the driver would get in the back and use large ice tongs to carry in a 25-pound or bigger block to put in someone's icebox. A card in a front window told the iceman if or how much ice was needed that week.

I had never seen an icehouse, so one winter evening, my father took me to the one by Hartford. Being around four or five, my memory of its location is faulty. We were down by Green River, and I watched men dragging blocks of ice as big as end tables. The ground was wet and slippery; it had to be or the wooden skids or sleds the blocks sat on wouldn't have moved. Men hauled them up ramps into the icehouse for storage until summer.

Dad told me the large blocks were cut from the river when it froze over.

Inside the icehouse, the blocks were covered with straw or sawdust to help insulate and slow down the melting. I remember the place was cold and damp, and even though the men were dressed warmly, their clothes and shoes got wet. Dad's shoes and mine were very wet from just walking around. My feet hurt from the cold. My father offered to let me sit on one of the ice blocks, but I was cold all over, and sitting on ice would have made me colder still.

I remember wanting to leave, but my dad wasn't ready to. He had some business with one of the men there; maybe he was looking for work. He put me in the car, and turned on the motor. I was shivering, and the heat felt so good. I fell asleep quickly, and don't remember the ride home or being put to bed. I just remember the greenish cast of the dim lights from lanterns and bare light bulbs, the chilling dampness, and many men talking and working quickly.

It looked like rough work when I think back on it. The men had to wait until the winter temperature was cold enough for the water to freeze hard, and thick-enough to walk on and hold the sawing equipment. I don't know if they cut the blocks during the day or just at night. I also don't know if they moved the blocks to the icehouse by day or only by night. Dad did say that it was colder at night and there was less melting to work then.

But what I did learn from that visit was an appreciation for how easy it is to get ice today. I push my glass up to the door dispenser and push; out comes either crushed ice or cubes, my choice. Sometimes though, I think about what I saw as a child in the 1950s. It was a cold job I wouldn't have wanted.

Daddy Didn't Leave

"I think I'm losing my mind," Mother said and buried her face in her hands. She sobbed. "I keep seeing Brad out of the corner of my eye, and I know he's dead. His smell is still on his pillow. I hold it and breathe it when I go to sleep. I smell his cologne in the house some-times. Two weeks ago, I was looking out the window, and I saw him walking up the drive to the house. I tried to get up to go outside, but he disappeared. No one was there when I got to the door. I know it wasn't Brad, but whoever it was had clothes on like his."

All I could do for the moment was let my mother exhaust herself. She wasn't ready to be reasoned with, nor was she ready for an expla-nation. My father died in October. It was now May, and she had come to my house for a three week visit.

Mom was crushed when my father died of lung cancer. The doctor had told her that he only had, at most, six weeks to live. Somehow she convinced herself that he had six months; she was in denial. Daddy lasted only three weeks.

After the funeral, I had to return home, and my mother gave up. She simply sat in a chair waiting to die so she could be with him. She wouldn't eat unless someone brought her food or took her to the gro-cery and made her shop. Even then all she bought were Cokes, Ensure, and TV dinners.

She was living in Florida, and I was in Indiana. There was little I could do to soften her depression. I knew she liked to read Gothic mystery novels and modern murder mysteries so I enrolled her in two book clubs. When several books arrived at a time, I checked to see if they were what Mom would like, paid the bill, and sent the selections to her. Others not selected were sent back. She was assured of at least five or ten books a month to read. These and television occupied her time.

I anticipated my mother's behavior some 18 years earlier. Dad and I finally managed to have some time to talk when Mother wasn't around, and the topic of death and the hereafter came up. We discussed our beliefs and found we were on common ground. Then the subject of Mother came up. She would never talk about dying or what she believed in so both of us could only guess. We did come to the conclusion that she would be helpless if Dad died first, so I asked my father to make me a promise. I wanted him to come back when it was her time to die; to be the first person she would see and to not be afraid of the future. He could escort her through the light and tunnel. I didn't want her to hang back out of confusion or fear, and not cross over. She could be trapped here as a ghost. Her house would be sold and she would have no one. He agreed that if he could come back, he would.

Listening to her tell me of seeing my father, I knew it was time to discuss that promise made long ago. I fixed her some hot tea as she would not have any soup, sat down near her, took a long breath, and began what I was sure would be a difficult discussion. I was surprised. She didn't sneer and wave me away as if disgusted by my words. She didn't get up and go into another room.

She listened, actually listened to me, as she had never done before. She was quiet when I told her of the discussion and promise made so long ago. I explained that Dad was just trying to let her know that he was still around, and hoping to comfort her.

"You aren't losing your mind, Mother. Dad is really here. Talk to him and acknowledge that you know he's here whenever you smell his cologne or see him. Don't try to pretend that what you see or smell or even hear isn't real. Don't push Dad away, or he will leave in frustration."

She was silent after the one-sided discussion. She just looked at the floor. I didn't know what she was thinking. She just asked what was for supper and could she have some more tea? She picked up my book on Henry Tudor, which she had been reading, and settled back into the same chair where she had sat for the past two weeks. She only left that chair to eat, to use the bathroom, and to sleep.

One week later, my husband and I drove her to the airport for her trip home. The discussion wasn't mentioned again. Maybe it helped some because that fall she bought tickets for a cruise to the Canadian Rockies. She and Dad had planned to take that vacation; now she decided to go with a companion. She did call to tell me she was going, and cried because my father wouldn't be with her. I felt that she was on the mend finally.

When Mother returned from the trip, she seemed happier. She called to tell me all that had happened. She had taken pictures and send duplicates to me. She joined in the activities down at the recreation hall in her neighborhood, and was excited that my daughter and I were coming for Christmas. She had made some ornaments and a perpetual calendar out of plastic mesh and yarn for Erin.

Then she tripped over the water hose out on the car port and fell on the concrete. She wouldn't go to the doctor, simply thinking she had bruised her hip badly. She could hardly hobble to the bathroom. She slept sitting high in her chair. When she finally did get coerced by her friends into going to the doctor, he told her that if she had come to him sooner, he would have pinned the hip as it was broken, and she was 76 years old. However, he then said it was mending quite nicely, and it should be completely healed in another two weeks. He told her to go home and continue doing whatever she had been doing that healed the hip. She did.

She even called me laughing about what the doctor had said. She told me that she felt better, the pain was gone. We talked about what to have for Christmas dinner, and I agreed to take her grocery shopping when Erin and I arrived. I told her that I was going to mail her present and for her to be on the lookout for a big box.

I had bought her a stained glass floor lamp for her living room. She seemed excited about the plans. We were going to get the tree out and decorate it. Just before she ended the call she said, "I saw Daddy again. He walked right up to the door, then I smelled his cologne in the living room with me." That's all she said on the subject.

Three days later, I received a call from the North Fort Myers sheriffs department notifying me that my mother had died in the kitchen. She had managed to dial 911 before she collapsed on the floor, phone still in her hand. She had had a massive heart attack.

I remembered asking Dad long ago to come back when it was time for her to die, to be the first person she would see when she left her body. The fact that she told me about seeing him only three days before I received that shocking phone call made me realize that my father had kept his promise. He did return and this time he came into the house and waited. Daddy didn't leave her to die alone, and I know he took her with him.

The Glassblower

The glassblower toils long hours in place.
Propane and other tanks litter his space.

A hot blazing torch heats glass at his bench;
big things and little he shapes inch by inch.

Dragons, dolphins, and dachshunds he creates,
and shimmering toppers for wedding cakes,

Hummingbirds and fays with pink golden wings,
octopi, bottles, pipes, jewelry, and rings.

He fabricates colors and knows their ways
to mix with clear glass and not crack or craze.

Cinderella's coach he forms with glass lace
while sweat travels down his weatherworn face.

His shoulders are aching; his arms are all burned
from creations fair he's fashioned and turned.

"An angelfish please, but make it all clear;
I'll paint on color, your price is too dear."

"Give me your secrets and teach me your skills.
I'll leave you no cash to give to your bills."

He carries his cases from store to street.
His wholesaled wares sellers want too cheap.

Been forty-some years of hard times and ease,
now sadly his art's remade overseas.

"I'll send a check later," shopkeepers say;
They'll take a long time if ever they pay.

With credit he buys more glass for his art.
It's filled his whole life, so deep in his heart.

The glassblower works long hours in place,
while sweat travels down his weatherworn face.

Dragons and dolphins and Dalmatians he makes,
and shimmering toppers for wedding cakes

PAM RAIDER

Pam Raider has resided in Brown County for 25 years and cannot imagine living anywhere else. Since retiring, she has continued social working by volunteering in many endeavors. Although born in the Midwest she was reared in California experiencing campus unrest during the Vietnam era. Those experiences colored her thinking which is still evident in her writings. For over fifteen years she was editor and contributing writer to the *Brown County Reflection Rag* and she credits her fellow writers Davie Ericson and Wanda Brown with honing her writing skills. She has been published in *Branches Magazine* and is a regular attendee of W.R.A.P.S. and their workshops. Currently she is stretching her writing skills by acting as managing editor of Brown County's new radio show airing on WFHB called the *Brown County Hour*. She feels writing has been a window into the interior life and thus leads to the Examined Life.

Moonflowers

Two moonflowers bloomed this night,
waiting only for the moonlight
to show themselves big and bright
tho' secret, wishing to be out of sight

Two moonflowers dressed in lace
before the moon rising in space
could shed upon us her grace
they showed their lovely face.

Two moonflowers in twilight
not caring for wrong or right,
not having to kill or fight
or win each other with their might

Two moonflowers bloomed this day
it seemed to me they wanted to say
no one path can have its way
partnership is here to stay

Two moonflowers not in a race
simply blooming at their own pace
wafting a slight fragrant trace
gracing this my lovely place

Two moonflowers tonight remind
we are of course all one kind
of this we must not be blind
and seek our neighbor to bind.

Two moonflowers stand for you and me
dancing round I am also thee
wanting now to live and see
how it is to create a We.

Two moonflowers blooming in the dark
as I venture out on evening lark
to unity they seem to hark
and in my heart they leave their mark.

Our Place in the World

A friend spoke of the grief she felt each day over the state of the Earth's ecosystem — species disappearance, poisoned air and water, melting ice caps — the litany we've heard. She felt helpless to change the course we are on.

Musing on her question, I saw a connection with the topic of legacy. She was speaking of the collective legacy we inherited and the collective legacy we will pass on. While individuals inherit DNA which determines certain traits and tendencies, all are born into a particular time and place, thus subject to the fashions and dictates of the times, culture and family we inhabit. We are inheritors of what has come before, good and bad. Are there things we can do to improve our circumstances? Yes, AND — it might make no difference in the physical outcome. If we are maimed or if our country is struck by disaster, we may not be able to change the facts. This does not keep our lives from having deep meaning or far reaching impact.

Seeing how things are might actually be a first step toward psychological sanity, especially if those around us remain blind to reality. Accepting the truth of our situation is not pessimism, but realism — a kind of clarity of vision which allows us to ask deeper questions. The most important of which seems to be given the situation in which I find myself, how do I respond, in the here and now, moment to moment?

This is the same question every person, whether conscious of it or not, is ultimately asking. And their actions and life story is the response. It might also be true that the more confined or limited the reach of the individual, the more intense the question becomes, since distractions are lessened. Would Helen Keller have become such an inspiration if she were not so limited? Stephen Hawkings became an astrophysicist in large part because his brain became the most functioning part he had.

In the same vein, perhaps the world crisis is a kind of gift. For now the stakes are higher and as the evidence mounts and becomes more undeniable, we must face ourselves and ask what kind of species we are. What values do we uphold? Are we human kind — both humane and kind? Or are we mostly concerned with getting our piece of the pie? Do we work to make the world a better place? The answers to these questions will determine the collective legacy we pass on, for the answers to these questions will decide the form our institutions take and the direction we move in the future.

Tomorrow's Flowers Grow From Today's Seeds.

A quote from my hippie days T-shirt.

Time / No Time

Hurry here, scurry there
Rushing 'round everywhere
Wish I could take more care
Gonna be late, can't hesitate
No time to deliberate.

I figured out the score
Gotta do a little more
Just another small chore
For if I do not make haste,
It's a big time waste.

Wait — a thought stops me cold,
You can put it all on hold,
Not just do as you're told.
What is this inner-voice
Timely reminding me of choice?

Red White Blues

RED
Color of the original people
Seeing red, the war god's favorite color
Red blooded Americans
Waving flags
Valentine hearts
Painted fire engine red

WHITE
Light skinned invaders
Pure pristine morals
Like new fallen snow
Obscure white lies
Clean Arab dress
Blows in the desert winds

BLUE
Blue blooded entitlement
True blue follows the leader
Beat them black and blue
Under cover of blue laws
Sunken, heavy hearted
Weary with sadness

Winter blues
Red blood
Spilt on white sands

This poem was originally written for a Poets Against The War event
in Brown County. I include it here because I revised it for the Libya bombing and
because I credit the process of this poem with my joining W.R.A.P.S..

Chaos Theory

Science used to believe in a mechanistic deterministic world. If we knew enough factors, we could predict anything. The advent of the computer and its ability to program multiple data to predict outcomes has proved this wrong. Edward Lorenz's weather pattern studies is credited with the discovery of what has become an interdisciplinary study called Chaos Theory. He is also the originator of the "butterfly effect" (if a butterfly flaps its wings in Brazil does that affect the weather in Texas?) Small variations in dynamic systems can produce large changes in outcomes. This has huge implications for the small fluctuations in world temperature which may produce huge unforeseen consequences.

In the film we saw, a mathematician demonstrated chaos experiments on a computer. The randomly programmed colors and times looked like flashes on the screen showing no order whatsoever. Yet, in a short period of time they organized into a very structured, tight pattern, like a kaleidoscope. Then, as if the pattern was too tight and had nowhere else to go, it broke down again into total randomness which later organized again into a pattern and broke down, on and on it went. Some modern scientists believe life evolves this way. In this dynamic evolution order breaks down into smaller pieces only to reassemble into another ordered pattern.

This theory may explain why all great empires break down. As they become too structured and ordered they cannot adapt to the changing forces confronting them. Local governments network, eventually organize into structured centralized government which becomes so hamstrung by bureaucracy it cannot respond to a Katrina-like event. Inevitably this centralized entity becomes top heavy and breaks down because there is no room for new solutions to emerge to confront the changing nature of life.

Perhaps it is foolish of us to think that one structure over time will satisfy all needs. Maybe cheap oil was a solution for a time, now changing realities call for new solutions. Once we lived under kings and dictators we worshiped as gods, now we move toward democracy.

What we have called natural laws (of life or the market place) may in fact be habits in a dynamically evolving process pushed on by creative adaptations that then become part of the next phase of habits.

Cultural norms may share these same characteristics. Language conditions the way we look at the world, beliefs are the lenses through which we see reality. If we are blind to the changes around us and adhere to the same old habits, we lock out creative solutions. The ability to adapt to a changing world requires cultural transformation which begins with creating a new dialogue. Change our minds, change our perception and a new world is possible. As a new way of viewing life, or rather viewing and explaining life, catches hold, a new paradigm emerges. Small changes shift whole systems. Where do new ideas come from? Is imagination and creativity something always available to us? Einstein and Edison took naps and their rational thinking was infused by creative thoughts. Perhaps all creation begins in chaos, progresses in chaos (because we resist change) and ends in chaos (when that order too breaks down). Chaos is not disorder but a gap between orders in which the transcendental attracts us toward a new and higher order of being.

Leaves in Pond · © Susan W. Showalter

DEBORAH CRONIN

Deborah K. Cronin was born in Western New York and grew up in Ashville, a small rural village located near Chautauqua Lake. Prior to retiring her writings included Christian books and articles published, most notably, by Abingdon Press, Upper Room Ministries, and The Church of Ireland. Of these, *Holy Ground: Celtic Christian Spirituality,* is best known.

Since retiring, Deborah has completed *Things Unseen,* a novel, and a non-fiction history, *Kiantone: Chautauqua County's Mystical Valley* (both available at www.authorhouse.com). Currently, Deborah is writing a collection of fictional short stories based on the annals of the Civil War era Indiana 27th Regiment, raised in Bloomington, Indiana, where Deborah now resides. She is also working on a lengthy group of (mostly humorous) short stories designed to look sideways at faith and life. Deborah may be contacted at 812-323-9615.

Angel Wings

For Bob and JoAnne

Bright
sunbeams
peeked through
the wooden blinds
stirring my dream-filled
slumber on winter's morning.
Again the grief of friendship lost,
life vanished, loneliness suffocating,
trust gone,
sadness here.

Beloved
visits past
took me to my
special ancient friend,
she ten decades vibrant
and pushing for the eleventh.
No one visit was enough so I feasted
on repeated journeys to her mystic table,
savoring the repast that only refined wisdom,
intelligence, insight, knowledge, and compassion
could
offer.

Last
Christmas
did not disappoint.
We chatted of holiday
things like trees and gifts
and music and food and memories
so strong, so vibrant, so familiar that
one might easily think they formed in her
mind only yesterday, like new-fallen snow.
Good times.
Good gifts.

As
dusk
taunted
a blue sky day
she sat back in her chair.
Story-telling hour had arrived,
scenes emerging from her memory
full of mirth, sorrow, striving and caring.
Were this crone's stories ever disappointing?
No!
Never!

Once
again she spoke
of war-time hardships:
husband off to dentistry school,
two bright, active children to raise,
home-fires to keep burning brightly and
a busy school teacher's job to pay the bills,
always told with hoarded bitterness because
it was a time when nothing came easily nor quickly.
All so hard,
hard, hard.

Stories
of world war,
battles still raging,
but freedom the goal
for those ensnared in death,
the first rays of triumphant dawn
stealing across cherished *Liberty's* heart.
In *Victory's* hope her family came to celebrate
the *Manger Child's* promise of ever-lasting peace.
Not yet,
but soon.

They
gathered that
hope-filled holiday
at her parent's rural home;
her brother and his family, too.
Mother had cancer and everyone knew
this might be Mother's last Yuletide celebration,
though no one would dare speak such thoughts
for fear that the words would too soon come true.
One hopes
in such times.

Pie,
pumpkin,
was a menu tradition.
Mother made the pie shells,
manna woven from flour and lard,
but had no strength for coring, peeling,
boiling, and mashing the bright orange gourd.
So Father went to the store and bought the family's
first can of pie filling which they all secretly thought was
work-saving
but wrong.

Later
that wintry night
her brother and his wife
with two young sleepy daughters
and a new baby girl bundled tightly
set off through the snow and ice for home.
My friend bedded her sleepy family in the attic
and then glimpsed her parents' sweet good-night kiss
before they went to separate bedrooms, surrendering to
cancer's scourge the intimate blessing of slumber shared.
Each slept.
Each dreamed.

An
hour or two
after midnight
she heard her mother
rise and go to the bathroom.
She went quietly to her mother's bed,
waiting to tuck her back under the quilt.
Mother smiled when she saw her daughter and
said, "Sit here for awhile; I never go back to sleep
quickly nor
easily."

They
told stories of
Christmases past
and present and the
(did they dare say it?)
hoped-for dawn of peace.
Pausing a moment to think,
 Mother said, "I may not be here
when Al graduates from dental school
in May. Please tell him how proud I am of him.
I am sure you will have a long and good life together."
And then
Mother slept.

My
friend
slept, too.
When she woke,
Mother was gone.
In one crystalline moment
the Christmas angel's miracle
was accomplished, bringing eternal
healing peace to Mother's diseased body.
The gift
of sleep,
of rest.

My
ancient
friend sat back
in her chair, ending
the story-telling hour.
She knew that wintry day
 that she would leave me just
as quickly and swiftly as her mother
departed
from her.

I
joyously
wished her
 a happy birthday
one sunny August day,
giving her a balloon bouquet
that brought a big grin to her face.
A few days later, my cell phone rang;
 speaking too gently, her niece told me
that my one-hundred-and-five-years-old
friend
was gone.

It
seems
Christmas angels
can transform our lives
any given day of the year.
Those are not comforting words;
they do not assuage or lessen my grief.
I want one more afternoon, one more story from the
ancient friend I held so dear. One more perfect story.
But, if she was here she would have none of my self-pity.
With her cantankerous angel radiating brightly, she would say,
"Get up! Go find another story! Go find your own angel story!"
I will.
Tomorrow.
I must.

The Scream

Attending the *Ropewalk Writers Conference* in New Harmony one summer was a bit of a stretch for me. But it turned out to be, if not the most entertaining writing experience I've encountered, then certainly in the top five.

The participants were largely city folk who thought coming to a Wabash River town founded by utopian-minded 19th Century pioneers was about as exotic as one could get in the Midwest. What they had not counted on were the June floods. By the time *Ropewalk* began, New Harmony was swarming with National Guard sandbaggers, MRE wrappers tossed everywhere, and a snake population that didn't like their habitat being disturbed and were out in force on the streets and sidewalks in serpentine protest. My dog did not like that one bit. Long after we returned to the sidewalks of Bloomington he would jump two feet into the air whenever he found a stick in our path.

As for me, I found the writers exotic. There was the young man from New York City who thought he looked like a young Nicolas Cage, though I am not sure why anyone would think that was a good thing. One woman was a harpist, which seemed lovely, until I realized that all her writings had something to do with that angelic instrument and sex. A very sweet-natured young man of Pakistani descent, a self-described professional poet, wrote intricate poems that resembled oriental rugs. Another older man presented nothing memorable in the writing workshops. But I do remember, more vividly than I wish, his mealtime singing of obscene lyrics to the tune of *There Is Nothing Like a Dame*. I am not sure, but I don't think that worked for him.

Certainly, one of the most colorful characters was the young woman who couldn't afford housing, so she tent-camped each night in the town park. I was staying with friends in their home, so several times I invited her to pack up her tent and crash on their couch. Each time she declined. On the last day or two I finally realized she was doing more than camping in the park.

This same young woman had various tattoos. She always wore halter tops and one tattoo peeked out shyly from her cleavage. I wasn't sure just what it was, but one day, as she bent over to hand a paper to an instructor, the tattoo boldly appeared. It was a large semi-colon. At first I wasn't sure that I had seen what I had seen, but later, when I asked the instructor about it, she began to chuckle.

Once she stopped chuckling, she explained that she had asked the young woman about that particular tattoo. The woman was quite open and said she had the tattoo placed on that part of her body to remind herself that a semi-colon is used when have two clauses of approximately the same weight both pointing in the same direction. Later, the husband of the couple I stayed with told me that word about the semi-colon tattoo spread like wildfire around New Harmony, with the local good 'ol boys regularly reporting recent sightings of it when they gathered for coffee at the Main Street Café.

But, the most interesting writer, by far, was another young woman. She was tall, slim, and red-headed. We're talking Lucille Ball here in the days before she became a comedian. Somehow, doing comedy moves women out of the beautiful category into the attractive category, something I have never quite been able to understand.

Anyway, in addition to this young woman's good looks, she was also bright. Real bright. Real intelligent. Real smart. The scary type of bright that makes you just want to smack her. She had brought along a lengthy poem she'd written about Vincent Van Gogh committing suicide. She had done extensive research and produced a tapestry of Van Gogh's life and work, including his favorite paint colors, his failed attempt to become a priest, and his various paintings.

On the day she read the poem to the writing workshop about twenty of us were seated around a large conference table. Babe, my miniature schnauzer, was under the table. After almost a week folks were comfortable with him and told me to let out his leash so he could wander around, getting more than his fair share of petting. Like a child bored with his mother, the dog was enjoying this special freedom.

Although I still had the leash in my hand, I had actually lost track of where Babe was. But after several pages of the young woman's elegant poem about Vincent, and just as she read the words, "the mind of God," Babe brushed his beard over her sandaled foot and up her bare shin.

Startled, she let out a shriek that echoed off every brick wall in New Harmony, causing young children to go deaf and Fundamentalists to drop to their knees thinking it was the Second Coming. If New Harmony's famed Roofless Church had stained glass-windows, her scream would have shattered them.

In an instant, I knew there was only one proper response I could make to this situation. Right on the spot I began apologizing profusely: to the young woman, to God, and to Vincent Van Gogh.

Lenten Delight

It's not often you can fit both J. S. Bach and Hell into one evening. But a Presbyterian pastor, a Congregational pastor, and a rabbi held a Lenten discussion series about their various faith perspectives with an organ concert preceding each discussion. I know it sounds like one of those jokes — two pastors, a rabbi, and a church organist were in a rowboat — but let's not go there.

My miniature schnauzer is a big NPR music fan so I decided to take him with me that evening. I know — two preachers, a rabbi, an organist, and a schnauzer were in a rowboat — but we're not going there, either.

The organist performed Bach's *Passacaglia in C Minor*. Each variation of the brooding, sturdy theme revealed that this was no phoned-in performance. The organist was at the top of his game. His rendition was lush and smothered in highly developed God-given musical talent. As the organist approached the masterwork's climax, it occurred to me that Bach was in the room, not literally, but more like a felt awareness of the composer cheering from some celestial balcony. It wasn't only Bach's cheering that filled the room; it was his creative joy. It flooded the room with delight. Could anything that was, or is, or is to come surpass such musical joy? You could feel it on your skin and in your teeth. Anyone who missed it simply didn't know squat about Bach and his music.

I've always wondered what Bach did after completing such a wonderful composition. Did he go down to the local *bier stube* and hoist a foaming lager? Did he go to the village *wine stube* and sip his favorite wine? Or did Bach just go home where his wife scolded him for forgetting to buy more candles or neglecting to pick up his new boots at the cobbler's shop? One wonders.

After the too brief organ concert, which my miniature schnauzer enjoyed immensely, the three clergy began their discussion about the topic *d'jour,* namely, do Jews embrace the concept of Heaven and its dark cousin, Hell? Grasping their theological rapiers they oh-so-politely saluted each other and then attacked and parried, reprised and parried again while still being very cautious so that neither would inflict any serious wound on the other's theological armor. The two pastors politely noted that *Sheol,* a concept something like life after death, slowly developed in Judaism, as witnessed by the Old Testament. But the rabbi did not take the bait, preferring, I guessed, to see just how deep a hole the Protestants could dig for themselves.

It was soon obvious that no one, given their reluctance to attack seriously the issue at hand, was going to be declared the victor in this theological fencing match. This was a good thing, since up to that point none of them had inflicted any fatal theological damage on those in attendance that evening. Unfortunately, they then decided to open the floor to anyone who felt compelled to express his or her thoughts about Heaven and Hell. Big mistake.

The result was a torrent of banalities, clichés, and trifling comments. The worst of these came from a middle-age woman who said she had grown up in a town that lacked a Jewish population. When she went to college she encountered Jews for the first time in her life. One Sunday morning a Jewish girl who lived in her dorm invited her to go out for bagels, lox, and cream cheese. As she said those words, I stopped breathing, fearing what she might say next. How bad could this get? Well, worse than I could have possibly imagined.

The woman spoke rapturously about her first taste of the chewy bagel, the salty goodness of the lox, and the smoothness of the cream cheese. In a final self-satisfied conclusion, she announced that in that not theological moment, but, rather, culinary moment she realized that Jews were good people after all. As she sat down, I began to pray feverously that the earth would just split open and devour us rowboat and all. But God wasn't paying any attention to my prayer. Most likely, God was too busy figuring out how to get the woman to try *sushi,* stuffed grape leaves, *foi gras,* and fried locusts. Who knows what spiritual insights could come from ingesting those delicacies?

Finally, an elegant, tall, dark-haired fifty-something woman seated in the back row rose to her feet. Her stately presence caused a hush to fall over the room. With steady, deliberate speech she said,

"I am Native American. I was born into a family that practices traditional Native American spirituality. Twenty years ago a friend invited me to this church and I became a Christian. I still love my Native American relatives that believe differently than I do and I know they love me, too. But if I told them about what has been discussed here this evening, this question of who is going to Hell and who is going to Heaven, I know they would ask, 'Isn't that up to God to decide?"

I was sitting near the woman and could not contain myself any longer. But it was obvious that my "Yes!" and "Praise the Lord, Sister!" made everyone in the rowboat feel uncomfortable.

That night I dreamt that I visited an exciting, growing church. The greeters at the door invited me first to go downstairs to the basement. There the church members had set up numerous interpretation booths about the congregation's various missions and ministries. There was also a food court displaying all kinds of good things to eat. I planned to visit the booths, sample the goodies, and then return upstairs to worship.

Suddenly the church basement was filled with flying monkeys. In my dream I became convinced that I could not go upstairs to the sanctuary until I cleaned up all the flying monkey poop, of which there seemed to be an endless supply. As soon as I cleaned one mess, another flying monkey made another one.

I hope. I hope. I hope Bach plays the organ in Heaven. As for Hell, well, maybe Hell is just this: eternally cleaning up flying monkey poop, so deep you could float a rowboat in it.

Brown County Snow · © Jude Edwards

PAIGE ARNHOLT

I was born in Seymour, Indiana November 15th, 1995. I lived in Seymour until I was ten. The bank for-closed on our old house as my parents were divorcing. My mother took us to a shelter for a few weeks. My mother then moved us into my grandmother's house in the country where we lived for two years. While there, my aunt Carolyn practically raised me. Mom worked a lot and my brothers stayed with dad on the weekends. Aunt Carolyn taught me many life lessons.

She taught me how to count money, write poetry, and not be afraid of people. She also took me to W.R.A.P.S. (Writers, Readers & Poets Society) at age nine. I have been a member for seven years. With W.R.A.P.S. and my aunt teaching me, I've come to realize the importance of writing and respect through them.

When I was twelve, mom found a house just up the street from my grandmother's where we have lived since. I march in the school band and act in 'Destination Imagination' (DI) and am in the FFA (Future

Farmers of America). I have discovered that Matthew and Michael aren't my only siblings. I have nine brothers and sisters through my father. Some I haven't met yet. I am the only one of these who write and joins a lot of school activities. I am also the youngest member of W.R.A.P.S.

Blind Love

Would you love me more if I dyed my hair, or would you like me less if I lost weight? Would you still lust after me, if I stayed the same, would you be satisfied If I were to risk my life for you, give you my heart, tell you my darkest secrets, and cherish your every kiss, would you handle my love with care or would you be like the others and through blind eyes, toss me away?

Lost Dreams

My black fingernails seem to crack with the chilly cold untouched and unheld. My skin grows icy, tinted blue, my lips frost bitten and forgotten, my heart neglected, quiet, with no one to give it a reason for which to beat. My voice breaks away as I try to choke out these simple words, those three tiny words. Those words you never returned. Then the raspy sound of my voice falls and shatters on the snowy ground. I again fade away back into the darkness, back into everything I know. You, my lost long forgotten dream.

ERIN BOWDEN

Erin-Jada Bradleigh Bowden has been singing since she was very young and began singing professionally in middle school. She has won many awards for her voice, including six gold medals, one silver medal, two plaques, and a trophy for best musical actress.

In June of 2008, her first CD, *LostAtHeart,* was released; containing thirteen original songs, all written by Erin herself. There are techno songs, inspirational songs, even a pirate shanty, and a spiritual piece dedicated to her mother, Mary Deborah Bowden, whom she thanks everyday for her constant support.

Aided by her electric piano, everything on the album that is not guitar work or drums, (save for the electronic percussion featured in *Love of a Soldier and Dream of a World*) she played and recorded herself.

Now graduated from Ball State University with a major in theater design technology and minor in creative writing, Erin is now pursuing a BA degree in Creative Writing. Currently, she has enough material for her second album, Equinox, and has already begun recording.

In addition to her music, Erin is also an author. She plans to go to Georgia State for a Masters of Fine Arts in creative writing so that she can teach writing at a university. She hopes to follow in her mother's footsteps one day and publish a book of her own. She says that her love of writing and story telling stems from the stories that her mother used to tell her when she was little. Currently, Erin has several poems published in her mother's book *Dandelions and Other Weeds,* and in another book, *Treasured Moments,* a compilation by Sue Breeding. She has contributed stories to two magazines: *The Realm* and *Pen-It* and has done illustrations for the children's book *The Sack Lunch,* and cover art for *Dandelions and Other Weeds* also by her mother. She is the coauthor of five children's books: *Horus, the Misunderstood Buzzard.* Book one, *Horus Has a Problem* is soon to be published.

While she works on her own original stories, Erin loves to write fanfiction on the side. Many of her pieces, as well as a few original poems and short stories, can be found at her online art profile at www. skippy-the-demon.deviantart.com.

Copies of *LostAtHeart* are for sale in The Book Loft in Nashville, Indiana and also through Erin herself or her mother, Mary Deborah Bowden.

Anam Cara Mine

Sister mine, yet not by birth
Stranded, separate, walk the earth,
until, elate! Found once again!
Aman Cara, Sister, Friend.

A soul to match, a pair unborn
Unseen hole where none should be
Spirit, soul resplendently
patched and fixed, and now made one,
unaware we'd been undone.

Hands clasped in trouble, hardships, pain,
sorrow, strife, grief, and gain.
Hearts bound in shadows brief, and light,
twin spirits walking through the night.

Body Language

"Hold me," his eyes said, so she did,
"Stay," said his arms as they held her in place,
"I love you," was there, just past his lips
 though he needn't have said it;
 it was there on his face.

Interlocked fingers and a whispered kiss
 and time stands still, as it should.
'Till one day her eyes and her lips would both speak;
"Hold me," she said
 and hold her he would.

The Marionette

There was a marionette in the hall today. She was slumped against the wall, just sitting near the stairwell. As I walked by, I saw that her face was chipped and cracked, her paint faded, and her smile worn away. Threadbare were her clothes. Tattered strings adorned her hands, like manacles still. A pretty slave clapped in irons.

I stopped to look at her. She slept, and would not wake for all the world. So I kissed her painted eyes and bid them open.

And thus she saw me.

"Why do you hide in the stair here, fast asleep as death and all alone?"

She told me then, in a voice that echoed the pale china on her lips, of how all her life she had danced until she cried and then danced on. Danced until she stopped dreaming. She told me then, of how she wished to be real and to exist within reality. Of how she wished for her puppeteer to cut her free. She told me then of how she defied the dance and tore away her strings from her master's hands and fled. And she told me then of how she found her way here — to the hall where all things dreaming must come to pass between the worlds, and slumped against the stair.

Too tired, was she, to climb up until she reached the lands of Far Away.

Her tale done, I took her hand into my own and pledged to carry her to the landing, where she could better stand. I took my blade from my side and cut away her strings, took my brush from my bag and painted her eyes to shine like new. And thus she saw me. Saw me truly.

We saw each other.

And her lips twitched as I painted her smile back into place — no longer false, no longer sewn on. A painted smile, and a smile that was for me and me alone.

I carried her, in my arms I held her close to me. And at the door to the lands of Far Away, I let her go, but she did not turn from me to leave.

She told me then, that she loved me.

And I kissed her pretty china lips, my pale and pretty Marionette.

The Harlequin Boy

There was a harlequin boy in the hall today. He stepped lithely around the corner as I lay against the stairs. He stopped to regard me, and I saw that his shirt was threadbare, torn, only just held together with pins. His hands were calloused and bruised as he reached out to me — as no one else ever had. He smiled then, a smile that was neither forced nor false. Free was he. Tattered but free.

I felt him kiss my eyes as he knelt. And thus he touched me.

"Why do you bother with a ruined doll such as me?" I asked of him. "Why be kind to one with no use, no purpose?"

He smiled then, and this time it was sad. His tale was as my own, his pretty painted mouth forming words so sweet and sorrowful. He spoke of how, once, he stood still as a statue in a window, looking out onto the world. Day after day, said he, his painted eyes had watched the sun and moon and the stars go down and longed to see them for himself. How he wished that the glass would break. How he wished that he could climb away from his lonely existence and begin to be. He was a dream that had lost its dreamer. Forgotten was he, standing until his clothes and china skin began to turn to dust. And so he pounded upon the windowpane as hard as he could, until his hands bled and his body fell from the sill onto the floor.

And from where he had fallen, he picked himself back up and fled. He smiled then, as he told me of his journey to this, the hall where all things dreaming must come to pass between the worlds, and began to climb the stairs.

And he had found me on his way to the lands of Far Away.

His tale done, he took me into his arms and enfolded me in them. He pledged to carry me to the landing — a fellow traveler on the journey home. He took his blade from his side and cut away my strings, took his brush from his worn cloth bag and painted my eyes to sparkle like the stars. And thus he touched me, and I saw him truly.

We saw each other.

He smiled then, and gave my own back to me with his brush. At last, my smile was mine to give to whomever I wished. And I gave it to him.

He lifted me up, carried me up the stairs as he stepped with grace. At the door to the lands of Far Away, he let me down. I did not leave him. I could not leave him. Not he who had shown me kindness, not he who had carried me, not he who was as lonely as I.

I took his hands in mine and said that I loved him.

And he kissed me with his painted mouth, my tall and graceful Harlequin Boy.

Water

You are more beautiful to me
than the sound of water
as it trickles through the earth,
rushes over the ground,
through the grass
and across the stones that lie
in the river,
waiting
to be moved.

Picked up and tossed,
or loved,
by the water that I love,
which makes a sound like
starlight
and a wish, that
reminds me of you.

On a Cold Winter's Day

My sister, Shelly, died last winter. It was sudden, a sickness, they said. I didn't get to go to the hospital to say goodbye or anything. One minute I was there next to her in line for lunch at school, perfectly fine, and the next, she just...collapsed. Right there onto the cafeteria floor. Her teacher called the doctor and the ambulance came to take her away.

I tried to go with her, but they shut the doors in my face and I couldn't get in. So I had to wait the rest of the day until my parents came to get me. They never did. I walked home that day after school. Came home to an empty house. Sat and waited some more. Waited for hours and hours, and when Mom and Dad finally came back, looking solemn and grey, I asked what happened. They didn't answer me and I didn't try again just then. I tried later, though, but it still didn't work. No one ever tells me anything.

I remember being sad, confused, lonely. I wanted my big sister, but she wasn't coming home. Not that night, not ever again, they said. I wanted to go and see her in the hospital, but no one paid me any attention when I asked them to take me. No one ever does. It's okay, though, I guess.

The funeral was three weeks later. Mom and Dad sat right up front, all dressed in black. No one had spoken to me for the longest time — I think they were all too sad and afraid that I wouldn't understand or something. But I did, I did understand. They were more concerned with Shelly, lying still and cold in the coffin at the head of the room than they were with me. I still understand. But I don't understand why no one would even look at me. Nobody ever tells me anything.

The preacher stood up there at the pulpit, telling us all things about my big sister that he wouldn't have known, since Mom and Dad and the two of us never went to church. But that was part of his job, to tell us all about the dead people that sat like stone inside their wooden box-beds when it was their time to go. Shelly was a smart girl, he said, a rare, shining gem in a sea of darkness. I don't think anyone really got what he mean by that. I know I didn't. But then he started talking about the lord's love or something and I tuned him out for the rest of the day.

Later on, when the sun had started going down — even though it was only about five o'clock — and the rain had let up a little bit, we all threw dirt over the top of her coffin as they lowered it down into the ground. Or, at least, I did. Everyone gave dirty, scandalized looks. Like I had done something wrong. That's all right, though, Shelly was my sister and I'd throw dirt onto her coffin if I wanted to. Mom and Dad didn't even say anything, just jumped a little because they got startled by it and then started crying again. Mom already getting blurry-eyed and red-faced, hiding in Dad's warm woolen jacket.

Mom and Dad stayed long after everyone else had gone away, I remember that. The rain had stopped, but it was dark out and it got cold then. We really should have gone home. I waited over by the car for them but they didn't want to leave Shelly. I understood, I did, really. But it was late. I remember asking if we couldn't just come back tomorrow, but they didn't answer. No one ever pays any attention to me. So I wandered back to the graves and stood behind the big stone that had her name written on it. It made me too sad to look at it.

But then I heard somebody calling my name. "Joey!" she said, and I turned around to see where it had come from and there, by the trees, was my sister. She didn't look dead, she didn't even look sick. She looked just like I remembered her being — bright and cheerful and healthy. She had on her school clothes, not that stuff they had buried her in. She waved at me. So I waved back. I remember I tried to get Mom and Dad's attention, tried to get them to look, but they wouldn't even acknowledge me. I tugged on Mom's sleeve and she brushed me off as she dabbed at her eyes with her handkerchief. I started poking Dad in the side with my finger, but he just shifted out of the way and pulled Mom back against his side. "Dad, Mom, look! It's Shelly!" I said, almost yelling, but they just kept staring down at the tombstone and crying. I didn't care about it. No one ever pays attention to me, anyway.

When it was obvious that they didn't notice, I remember running around them both while flailing my arms in their faces. Still nothing. So you know what? I turned and ran away from them. I ran towards Shelly. Because I could see my big sister, and she wanted me to go over to her. So I did. And the two of us hugged and played tag and hide and seek even after it seemed like our parents had forgotten all about us and driven off into the night, gone home and left us all by ourselves in the grave yard. But that's okay. Because she held my hand and walked home with me. Smiling. Just like her old self.

We play together all the time now, just her and me, just Shelly and Joey. Like old times. Like nothing's changed. Mom and Dad don't even notice us when we stay up late and run around the house playing "pirates and Indians" - a game that we made up years ago together. The two of us used to love it. Now that our parents have lost Shelly - even though she's still right here, they just can't see or hear her like I can — they're getting a divorce and Mom's moving away. Dad's moving back in with his mother. I'm not sad, not really. Well, just a little, I guess. I can understand why they're doing it after all, they just can't handle the pain. There's just not anything left to hold the marriage together anymore. I understand, even if nobody thinks I do, if nobody bothered to say something to me about it. It's okay, really, no one ever tells me anything. But I've got Shelly now, and she and I aren't going anywhere. We're going to stay right here in this house, just the two of us. Forever and ever. And I like it that way. My sister, Shelly, died last winter. She died of a sickness, they said. Well, I got sick too. I died two years ago.

Raven on Goat Hill · © Susan W. Showalter

KEITH KELLY

Keith Kelly grew up on a Howard County farm, spent time in a factory to earn his keep, then counseling and the Peace Corps to pay his dues. He now lives in the Brown County hills where he reads, naps and sometimes walks in the woods and plays with dogs, cats and sometimes words.

A Human Being

Ask not what I want to do with my life;
Ask instead who I want to be in my life.

My teachers in this learning endeavor
Were Mr. Trial and Misses Error.
Sent into the world to do, I did.

Dived the forbidden cliff into the gravel pit.
Bought ponchos from Ecuadoran Indians
    with skins like nuts.
Hermited in Fijian huts.
Drank a Mississippi of gin.
Was savaged by a friend
And befriended by a savage.
Helped manage a polluting factory

Unwittingly.

Alas, doing the homework of Mr. Trial
    and Misses Error
Did not satisfy my life, however.
But all this doing taught me to—

Be a little daring.
Be sober, sane and sharing.
Be respectful of the world's traditions.
Be selective in my missions.
Befriend and trust but be not slipshod.
Be still and know I am not God.
Be not a human doing.
Do be a human being.

HENRY SWAIN

Henry (Hank) Swain is a long-time Brown County, Indiana resident and storyteller. The late Frank Hohenberger's *The Liar's Bench* photograph has often been used to portray the fact that some of the county residents were prone to exaggeration in the telling of their stories.

Swain was not a natural born liar but the many years of exposure to stretching the truth by some of his contemporaries has rubbed off on him. The malady has infected him through this persistent exposure and caused his understanding of truth to become unusually flexible.

Few writers of tall tales can lie as authentically as Swain. The hills of Brown County have a long history of producing genuine tall tales. Some have suggested it may be caused by something in the water. Others speculate there may be a genetic factor caused by perpetual generational fibbing.

Previous books by Henry Swain include *Leaves for the Raking* (2005), a montage of stories, essays, poetry and observations on the human condition, *Why Now?* (2006) detailing the evolution of a conscientious objector, and *Hank's Tall Tales and Harmless Exaggerations* (2012) a collection of tall tales and half truths.

The Light Within

The Religious Society of Friends (Quakers) has created some unique expressions to explain their beliefs to others unfamiliar with their practice. They frequently refer to the "inner light" or the "light within" This description refers to their belief that "There is that of God in every person."

Little is ever said regarding the brightness or wattage of this light. It must vary from person to person. For some highly regarded Quakers their light shines as a flood light that illuminates a large area. Some Friends have the mystical gift for prophesy. Their light would cast as a beacon. For most, I suspect, their illumination might be closer to the wattage of a refrigerator bulb.

In fact the thriftiest of Friends only open the door when they feel the need to check their spiritual path. When satisfied they are still on it, they shut the door and the light goes out. They are very conscious of the environment and want to conserve the power that makes the light. They might be designated "Green Quakers. "

I'm not certain they know if the light goes out when they close the door. They believe that it does. Few of us ever stay inside to check it out. I'm willing to take it on faith that it does. I take a lot of things on faith that I can't prove, like God.

I suspect the term "inner light" is a metaphor for some kind of universal energy or power that is available for our use. It may come from God or it may just be there. But it is there for everyone, and must be downloaded so that it can work through us to become of practical use to us and to others.

If there is that of God (or Spiritual Energy, if that better describes God for you) in every person, then I think we must also acknowledge that there is Evil in every person. This is an observable fact. I suspect this universal energy is neutral by nature and absent of conscience. Like electricity, it can warm a cold house or blow it up depending on how it is used. This comparison suggests our "inner light" comes with a switch, and that it is our finger and only ours, that moves the toggle.

Another interesting human factor, temptation, is thrown into this switching practice. Why is it that the seductive nature of temptation always appears so alluring and immediate, while its negative consequences appear so well camouflaged as to seem improbable?

We are constituted as creatures of reason and emotion. Temptation is the messenger that challenges us to keep the two in balance. This is a difficult task, for many of our emotional responses such as pleasure and fear is both glandular and natural.

This suggests that if we do not maintain a balance between our reasoning ability and our emotional desire for immediate pleasure, we may in a moment of emotional high, move the switch to our own detriment and plunge us into darkness.

Error is a given part of our nature. Is it possible to find the switch and it to restore the light again? I think it is, but it comes with a high interest penalty for the misspent energy used in the brief misguided choice. The process by which we restore our energy credit rating is called "Forgiveness." The choice not to make the same mistake twice is the path to wisdom.

Double Dribble

There was this man from Paris France
Whose problem was, he wet his pants.
Now you may wonder how this ends.
Well you see, it all Depends.

The Death of Sliver Sam Milo

(From the Brown County Democrat · July 3, 1938)

This *Brown County Democrat* story was the result of a most unusual accident. Sliver got his nickname because of his prowess in whittling and carving wood. He also was known for rope twirling abilities. It was his dedicated hobby and he could out-rope any man in the county.

His nickname "Sliver" came from the unique way he peeled the bark off saplings in little slivers when he fashioned a new cane. His reputation for cane making was legend in the community. The intricate carvings on the canes were so unusual he was able to market them in a local shop to be sold to tourists. It was the combination of his deftness with the knife combined with his rope-twirling that did him in.

His creative mind seemed to be at work best when he was resting. On this fateful, hot summer day, Sliver was sitting on his porch with a home-made beer in one hand, rocking with a slow rhythm in his own hand-made rocking chair. He observed that he should cut the weeds along the lane to his cabin.

The slow rocking had put him in a trance-like creative state. He didn't like the hard work of using a scythe. In an "ah ha" moment it came to him that he should combine his rope twirling skills with his whittling prowess. The result was a prototype of later invention we know as a Weed Eater.

Sliver fastened his carving knife near the end of his twirling rope. He was a cautious man and realized there might be a slight danger of being cut in the shins by the twirling knife as he envisioned how his invention would work in practice.

He went to his woodworking shop and cut in half lengthwise two empty gallon tin cans, after removing the top and bottom lids. By strapping them to his shins he had two layers of metal to guard against an accidental cut.

His invention worked just about the way that he had envisioned. The knife, spinning in a twirling loop, whacked the weeds much cleaner and easier than the scythe. He was having fun with his new invention and began to fancy that he should patent his idea. The more he thought about it, he realized that the only market might be other rope twirlers, of which in the general population, there really weren't that many.

Sliver made good progress down one side of his driveway until he came to an iron gate to the pasture. He tried twirling to the lowest level to cut the grass under the gate. He became over confident in his skill with his new machine. He misjudged the blade's clearance to the iron post that supported the gate.

The blade ricocheted off the post, cutting the rope in the process. The knife bounced off the iron post directly to Sliver's chest. He slumped to the ground, stunned at what had happened. His last thought before losing consciousness was, "I should have stayed in the rocker and had another beer."

Sheriff Brannon was puzzled by what he observed upon arrival at the scene. There was Sliver, lying on the ground with a knife in his chest, tin cans wrapped around his shins and three sections of his twirling rope scattered about and no sign of a scuffle. What to make of it? Was it suicide, an accident, or murder?

Sliver didn't have any serious enemies that the sheriff knew about. It wasn't like Sliver to commit suicide. But then, some of those cane carvings were pretty weird. Then there was the question of the freshly cut weeds on just one side of the lane with no scythe about.

An autopsy showed he died of a heart attack; the cause, knife penetration. Going through Sliver's cabin after the funeral they discovered what must have been the last cane he carved. Over the curved cane handle was carved figure of a man with a knife in his chest. To this day Sliver's death remains an unanswered mystery to many in the community who knew him. In 1989 Sliver's case was featured on *Unsolved Mysteries* program on TV.

Could any modern detective do any better than sheriff Brannon, if we could re-create the scene he found? Would today's advanced forensics be of any help? I doubt it. But a good detective with a vivid imagination could probably solve the mystery by wondering why the knife handle in Sliver's chest had a knot attached to it and a short piece of rope with a clean cut on its end. But only Sliver really knows what happened and he isn't talking. Well, that's the story as well as I remember it. I may have missed a detail or two, but I got the heart of it.

Closing The Door

There will come a time and place
when all of us come face to face
with Death.
We will find there at the end,
not a stranger but a friend.

The greeter standing at the door
tells me I should not deplore
the life I now must leave behind.
There is another life to find
behind the now closed tightly door,
a whole new world I must explore.

Always there will be regret
but memories let me not forget.
Now open please and let me through
so I can say goodbye to you.

Borders

Astronauts often use these words to express their emotions at first viewing the earth from space: awe, beauty, lonely, life and fragile. They remark on how much it resembles the mapping of the continents and oceans as we observed them on the globe on our fourth grade teacher's desk. A secondary reaction observed was that there were no borders outlining the different countries.

Poet Robert Frost in his poem *The Mending Wall* asks: "Before I built a wall I'd ask to know what I was walling or walling out and to whom I was like to give offense."

Walls, fences, or borders define a form of separation. The line of separation can be inclusive, exclusive, sometimes both and sometimes neutral. A farmer fences his chickens not only for his convenience but to keep them safe from predators.

Frost gives an example of neutrality: "There where it is we do not need the wall. He is all pine and I am apple orchard. My apple trees will never get across and eat the cones under his pines."

Walls like the Great Wall of China and the French Maginot Line were designed to keep people out and are examples of exclusion. Such walls historically have a record of failure and become landmarks of futility. Humanity seems designed not to be fenced in for long.

Most of us if we own property, rightfully want know where our borders are. Surveyors make much of their living establishing the true definition of otherwise vague borders. Lawyers derive part of their livelihood settling property line disputes. In earlier times judges occasionally required disputing farmers to each build a fence separated by the distance of one foot. They were called "spite fences." Stubbornness could sometimes be costly

In our small town where my formative years were spent, a widow lady with apparently little else to do, considered the property lines shared with her adjacent neighbors a matter of great importance. She had the surveyor place little wooden pegs in the lawn that could be mowed over. She made a fetish of keeping her portion of the lawn mowed to a different height than that of her neighbors. Perhaps her concern could be called a "spite lawn."

Some walls of exclusion become walls of discrimination. Our country is building a wall of separation with our neighbor Mexico. It is designed to keep people out. We have no such problem with our border with Canada.

Our Mexican wall is justified on the premise that people illegally enter and transport unwanted drugs into our country. Missing in this argument is, on which side is the demand for illegal drugs? On which side is the demand for cheap labor that brings high profit for those who exploit the vulnerability of the illegal workers?

Israel is building a wall of separation between it and Palestine and in the process is capturing some of Palestinian land illegally. Alas, wall builders seldom believe history will ever apply to them. It is the nature of humanity not to learn from history but to repeat it. Does it ever cross the minds of wall builders that their efforts will one day be considered tourist attractions?

The poet was right as he continues: "Something there is that doesn't love a wall, that wants it down." Of course, a wall has to be built before it can be torn down. Humanity has been quite competent building such edifices of futility. Wall builders, history ensures you will have steady employment and a prosperous future. So it will be for the builders of heavy machinery to tear them down.

Luck's the Joker in the Game of Life

When we are born into this world we are given a virtual deck of cards. It is our destiny to play the hand we are given. The game of life is fraught with great uncertainty. Some appear to have been dealt better hands than others. How do we explain this obvious unfairness?

Every new deck of cards contains an equal set of four suits; Clubs, Spades, Diamonds and Hearts. An extra card completes the deck. It is sometimes called the 'Wild Card' or 'The Joker.' It may be my imagination but I always thought the Joker had a smirk in his countenance.

Now, after over nine decades of living experience, I have come to believe the Joker represents the 'Luck Factor' in our lives. Herman B. Wells, distinguished president of Indiana University for many years, was asked to what he attributed his success? His answer was, "Be lucky." He even wrote a book about the luck factor in our lives.

The great puzzling question regarding luck is why do some have better luck than others? Some believe we make our own luck. To a degree that may be true. All choices we make have consequences. We all learn from the bad choices we make, or should. Making better choices should increase better luck in the outcome. That process isn't luck but rather the result of cause and effect.

True luck operates in a realm outside the law of cause and effect. Luck creates its own time table. Its distribution appears to be random and at times seems whimsical and other times malevolent. Is there a connection between luck and superstition?

Can good or bad luck be inherited? Some families apparently pass on to their descendents proclivities to certain diseases. This sticky unfairness indicates luck may have a mean side. Or does it? What then is luck? I believe luck is a form of energy and like all energy, a neutral force.

The great question then is who or what is the 'Great Distributor' of luck visiting us from time to time and who is the 'Great Chooser' of whether the luck will be good or bad? Is luck a part of the rhythms of our universe?

We never know when luck may come or what its nature will be. Is there a mathematical formula to luck? Often disaster-luck appears to come in sequences of three within a short space of time. There is no postponement of luck or announcement of its arrival.

It plays a significant part of our lives. Is there anything we can do to affect the quality of luck that comes to us? Does our attitude about luck affect the outcome? I like to believe so but can't prove it. As the Joker implies, luck is the wild card in our lives. All we can do when it arrives is to gratefully accept it if it is good and confront it if it is bad. For now, I wish you good luck.

KEITH BRADWAY

Keith Bradway grew up in the northeast part of Indianapolis and graduated from Arsenal Technical High School in 1944. He attended Purdue University and graduated with a BS in chemical engineering in 1948. Keith studied the science of pulp and paper making at The Institute of Paper Chemistry graduate school in Appleton, WI. He met his wife Rita there and they were married after he had finished two years. He obtained a PhD from Lawrence College as a result of his studies there. Keith worked for the Camp Manufacturing Co. in Franklin, VA in a technical capacity and later with its successor Union-Camp Corporation in Princeton NJ in research.

After his retirement in 1991, they moved to Brown County to a house his father had built on a portion of his grandparents' farm. Keith is a member of St. Agnes Catholic Church where he serves on the communications committee and in the choir. He is a member of the Brown County Widowed Group and the Writers, Readers, and Poets Society of Brown County. He enjoys working on his wooded property and playing golf.

The Imperative "Do"

I am uncomfortable with the use of the imperative "do." An example is the airline stewardess saying, "Do keep your seat belt fastened as we are taxiing and on take off and landing." Or the society matron's words to a departing guest, "Do stop in to see us the next time you are in the neighborhood."

The "do" of the stewardess is unnecessarily commanding; we know she speaks with authority. The society matron is trying to convince us of her sincerity, but it is overkill, and makes me suspect that she does not really mean it.

In spite of my complaints about the usage, I would not want it banned. I welcome the pleasure of that line from a Cole Porter song which reads, "Do do that voodoo that you do so well, for you do something to me, that nobody else could do."

On Limericks

The limerick's sounds give a thump
Sometimes like a slap on the rump.
But it's not just the rhyme
That makes it sublime
It's the bump dee dee bump dee dee bump.

This is not a Limerick*

Mr. Jones was apoplectic
when he saw his bill (electric).
Solar panels on his roof
will keep his manner more aloof,
And make his power more eclectic.

* The meter is not that of a limerick.

An Autumn Day

Along the road to Morgantown
a young boy rode his 'cycle down
the busy highway's double yellow line.

He'd seen his daddy go that way
that morning near the break of day.
He knew it was the path a man should take.

He did not know the peril there.
November's day was calm and fair.
The road's broad ribbon beckoned him to come.

A truck was hurtling round the bend.
Its driver scarce could comprehend
that tiny figure weaving on its way.

Behind the boy a trailing van
and pickup stopped. Each driver ran
to flag the ominous behemoth down.

The trucker braked, no coward he.
His big rig formed a treacherous vee
before it stopped, but stop at last it did.

A lady jumped down from the van
then to the spot she quickly ran
to seize and hold the wayward cycling child.

The errant trike was gathered in.
Its deadly race it would not win.
The rider's gallant quest had been denied.

The pickup driver pointed out
The place the young boy lived, no doubt.
To which the couple took the youngster back.

The semi started with a roar
As cars resumed their pace once more.
The day's tranquility had been restored.

That fateful day, as mother dozed,
A youngster, with the gate unclosed,
found Freedom's taste too sweet to be ignored.

But freedom's not so quickly found.
The young boy soon had met its bound
In strangers who had happened on the scene.

Was there an angel watching him?
Or was it just a chancy whim
That saved him on that autumn afternoon?

Have you not ridden Freedom's horse
along some strange forbidden course
and found yourself in trouble much too deep?

And have you gone a bridge too far;
Then found Hope's door was left ajar,
and through its narrow slit escaped once more?

Perhaps we live by throws of dice.
As storm-tossed as mere hulls of rice.
If God were choosing, why should he choose you?

The Empty House

I stop the car gratefully.
After the constantly curving twists
of route 45 from Bloomington;
Coming down from the hills
to Bean Blossom Creek.

And the long shady hall
of the railroad road.
I rush into the house.

It is late.
Supper must be started.

No one asks, "How was your game?"
Nor do I, the grump, answer,
"It wasn't a game.
I was only practicing."

Then no one asks, "How was practice?"
And I do not say,
"So, so, I guess."

A shelter for my disappointment.
Golfers never do as well
as they think they are capable of.

She only wanted to share.
Was that too much to ask?

Thoughts on Haiku

Haiku is a song
Fitting the Japanese style
Can English also?

I would like a Japanese person who is fluent in English to publish a CD or tape in which he recites Japanese haiku so as to give us a flavor of the sound of the rhythms which are said to be important to the language and to haiku. He would also translate the haiku into English so we would understand the meaning. I don't think the translations should have the same 5-7-5 syllable count as the original haiku, as the meaning may be clearer in a different combination of syllables. I think that would give us the ultimate feeling for the original haiku.

I wonder if English poets should try to use the 5-7-5 combination at all. Perhaps there is a better pattern for English, maybe 6-8-6 or some other scheme yet to be discovered.

Trying and Doing.

It is common to hear someone say, "I am going to try and do something." It is considered proper, but I would prefer that it be expressed as, "I am going to try to do something." Expressed that way it does not imply that the undertaking will be accomplished, whereas the first statement promises two things, first to try, and second to complete the task.

I think the first statement is improper, one cannot perform a voluntary action without trying and the declaration that one is trying is unnecessary. There are times when the trying is very important. Consider the statement, " I am going to try and quit smoking." We know that it is unlikely that the person will succeed. It is probably a lie to say that he will. When expressed as: "I am going to try to quit smoking," we can feel confident that he will at least give it a good try.

Winter

The "First Day of Winter"
one of my calendars announces.
Another says, "Winter Solstice."
I'm supposed to know
what that means.

Is it winter the whole day
having started at midnight
when many of us are asleep?
Or does it start
at some more convenient time?

Perhaps at noon
suited to late arisers.
Or at some mystic time
fixed by oracles.

I really need the answer;
It will tell me
when to start counting
each second
until it is over.

Modern Poetry

I make sense of it.
These words strewn around the page.
What meant they to him?

What do You Think?

Ambrose Bierce is quoted as having modified Rene Descartes' first principle of "I think, therefore I am," to make it say, "I think I think, therefore I think I am." Descartes would probably have been shocked at such a transformation. But the use of "think" is worthwhile; when a person expresses what he thinks he cannot tell a lie, no matter how many errors may have been involved in his thought process.

The use of "I think" is well suited to promoting discussions between antagonists which might otherwise turn into unproductive name calling or worse. Its use can soften everyday conversation. It says, "I might be wrong, but this is what I am thinking." One might say, "You're a liar," and receive a punch in the nose. The statement "I don't think that's true," would be much less provocative. In the words of a biblical proverb, "A soft answer turns away anger."

Is this being excessively wishy-washy, too much like Caspar Milquetoast of the comics? I don't think so, but I feel sure it would not be tolerated in most courts, especially not that of Judge Judy. She shelters herself in her robes to make statements like, "You're lying, Mr. Smith, and I find in favor of your opponent.

I think we can all benefit by moving our discourse in the direction of stating what we think and in saying that is what we think.

I, the Baker

Flour, sugar, yeast, oil.
Things to make a wholesome bread.
What about a heart?

Sounds from the Innocent.

Did you hear the worm?
He did not like the fishhook.
Nor the role he played.

Nursery Rhyme

Carolyn, oh Carolyn,
where have you been?
The people here at W.R.A.P.S.
want to hear about sin.

The things that the people
of Freetown may do.
Then she can recite them
for me and for you.

Song based on the nursery rhyme which begins:
"Suzie, little Suzie, oh what is the news?"

Old Barn in Winter · © Jude Edwards

JOHN MILLS

After 22 years of schooling (probably too much), I escaped academe to spend 26 years as the village potter in Nashville, Indiana. Then came seven years shifting seasonally between Colorado and Arizona as an itinerant potter selling at art fairs. While out West, often driving 500 to 1,000 miles each way to the fairs, I filled the time by writing down thoughts and images on 3 x 5 cards balanced on my knee. I like a plain spoken style, which I absorbed from reading my father's poems after he was gone.

At the end of 2000, we had a chance to return to the same house and shop in Nashville, as if we had never left. We **could** go home again and **did**.

Destiny

Issue of Abraham
from other mothers
A feud among brothers
or cousins

Is it a Poem

Is it a poem when it's spoken
or must it be in print?

The printed words and lines
have shape, unlike
the spoken ones.

But speaking them can shape the sounds
in ways the printed ones cannot.

Woman Walking

Skirts caressing
her energetic
stride

Curtained form
straining against
the cloth

A fleeting vision
of beauty in
motion

Fixed

I fixed something today.
The job went so smoothly
it felt too good to be true.

I had the right tools and hardware
and was able to find them.
Nothing else broke while I was working.
No surprises in the way it went together.

The quick completion felt like a refund of time
and compensation for all the other times.
I was so elated, I had to tell someone.
My wife seemed unsurprised.

Graceless

So long striving
against our adversary.
Then, surprise,
we are alone,
supreme.

Till hubris quickly trips us.
Who needs enemies?
We have ourselves.

Pocket Gem

Pocket knives are for men
as jewelry is to women.
Each time a knife is taken out
there's a reason for its use.

To cut a rope, open a box,
turn a screw, pry a little,
remove a splinter, or clean
and trim your nails.

At idle times
feel its form
in the bottom of your pocket.
Reason enough to have it there.
But, there's more.

Feel it in your hand,
the handle, the blade,
its shape and weight,
the action of the hinge.

Touch the edge.
Feel it nip, lightly,
at your skin.

Hold it to the light.
Admire the sheen of
the finely ground planes
that meet to make an edge.

Sight along the edge.
There's nothing to see.
Sharpness approaches ideal line,
a form that has no width.

Sharpening is another excuse for handling your knife.

The bright steel at the beveled edge
confirms the feel of a well honed blade
gliding across the stone, and
gives a momentary sense of diligence.

My father in law has asked for it
to do some minor task; but
really, I think he's testing me
to see if I've kept it sharp.

Small Town

I was a kid in the fifties.
We played ball in the street.
It was a town without much traffic.

Sometimes a neighbor called the cops
to quiet us and make us stop.

We paid him back
at Halloween.

Repetition

Repetition wasn't taught in art school.
We were supposed to ejaculate our ideas
into two or three dimensions.

Mimicking someone who had
recently been discovered,
while changing just enough to be original,
seemed to please everyone who mattered.

Later, I learned through practice
that repetition hones skill, confidence
and grace of line and form.

Enough of it frees hands from mind
and vice versa.

The mind can watch the form emerging,
assenting and guiding remotely, applauding;
while the hands do their work
unfettered, unerringly, unconsciously.

The masters, who we studied
knew this, I'm sure.
But, why didn't the professors?

Maybe they had never felt it.
They had a hint of it,
which they called style,
in an approving tone.

But, they seemed to sneer at repetition
if it fell outside of their
academically sanctioned categories.

Could I have heard, if
they had known to say it?
Or, did I have to feel it
to understand?

Would I have been encouraged
or would I have resisted?
Maybe I should thank them
for leaving it alone.

Potter's Poem

Pottery, sounds harder, more perfunctory.
No nonsense here.
The letters alternate consonants and vowels,
except for the extra "T."
A utilitarian word.

Poetry has a softer sound, more demure,
in keeping with its reputation.
The "T" and "E" have traded places,
throwing out the twin,
each joining with another of its kind.

They've quieted the "R" and
made the word sound breathy,

as I suppose it should.

Jobs

I've never had a real job,
with a boss, at least not
since the student jobs
and the domineering professors,
who exercised their power
much as bosses.

It wasn't planned,
not consciously at least;
but having had the feel of it,
I could never go back.

The risks work both ways.
Disappointments are more than balanced
when results exceed expectations.

It doesn't matter what I do
If I'm working for myself;
and working harder will
directly benefit me.

People who have never felt this
wouldn't risk the insecurity;
but if they ever tasted freedom… h'mm,
maybe we shouldn't tell them.

Simplest Thought

The simplest thought takes the longest to think.
When it comes it seems so clear.
Why did it wait so long?

Time taken to learn the questions,
to work them under your skin,
those are the years that pass
before you are ready.

When it comes you know.
The realization is instant and certain.
A cascade of confirmation rushes through your mind,
as you quickly check the fit with what you know.

The fit is good.
It's clear and easy.
Why couldn't I think of that
twenty years ago or thirty?

Because you weren't ready
to think of it
until now.

Take it Somewhere Else

Self-satisfied sympathizers
recite their inane blather:

It's a blessing in disguise.
The Lord has a reason for everything,
or similar claims.

I've always been patient with them;
but this is too much.

Felled at birth by a brain defect,
living only to a toddler's age
without toddling or doing anything else,
barely aware of his surroundings.

Everyone is supposed to get a chance.
He didn't get one.

Take your God
and your sanctimonious remarks
somewhere else.
My patience is gone.

The New Dark Ages

The dark ages seemed so jaded
when we learned about them
in school.

How could the powerful of that time
condone their self-serving
suppression of knowledge?

We dismissed it as the ignorance
of an ancient time, but
It's back.

Our leaders alter or suppress
studies that contradict
their policies.

Their dogma supplants research.
War continues, unsupported
by reasons.

Earlier contrarians
were silenced
by death.

We silence ourselves,
by inaction.

Wash Your Ears

Wash your ears every day
like your mother said.
Get out all that dirt.

What if seeds are hiding there?
Inside your ears it's warm
and damp,
right for germination.

If the sprout finds dirt enough
it could take root and stay.

When that sprout comes leafing out
you might decide to pluck it.

By now it's not just leaf and stem
but root ball on the end.

Depending on how long it's been
your brain may come out with it.

I'm sure your mother knew all this
She should have told you why.

But, now you know to wash your ears
and why.

JUDE EDWARDS

I grew up in northwest Indiana, and in 1989, enlisted into the Indiana Army National Guard. In 1990, I was selected for an active duty position with them, and retired with 20 years of active duty service in 2009. I also graduated with the Scholastic Award of Cum Laude and received an Associates Degree in Science in 2005, from Vincennes University.

In the late 90s I was transferred to Camp Atterbury, and relocated to the local community near it. As life would have it, I met my soul mate the month following 911. He just happened to live in Brown County, where I gladly moved to be with him. I am married to my soul mate who I consider to be a true gift in my life. I also have two wonderful daughters and son-in-laws, and have also been blessed with five darling grandchildren ranging in age from three to fifteen.

In my mid-twenties, prior to my joining the military I wrote and directed short skits for adult and youth groups at various community churches. Which also on occasions reached out into the local community.

During my troubled teens my dad {who I fondly call Pops} once told me that my problem was that "I think too much". (In all honesty

I believe that his parents said those same words to him in his younger years) I took his comment which he had said in sheer frustration as a compliment. Because "I think too much" I use my writing as a tool to address current events, plus to reflect and reorganize thoughts, actions, and feelings, and on occasion just for entertainment.

Besides being an avid rock collector from various parts of the United States, my mom {who I fondly call Mumzie} was also an avid photographer. I can not remember a time in my life without rocks and a camera being a part of my parents' household. I would say that Mumzie was a collector and documentor of memories, and Pops was witty with his spoken words. I believe that they both were a positive influence in my life, and I hope that even though they are no longer with me in this physical world that their "energy force awareness" is proud of their influence on me. Because, I too have a love for rocks and am always documenting the beauty of nature that surrounds us using the art of photography. I can only strive to be as witty as Pops was in documenting the world around me in using the art of writing.

I wish to say "Thank You" to Pops and Mumzie for their love, patience, perseverance and inspiration to my life. I can only say that they would also be proud to see that I have risen above the adversities and life insanities that have plagued my adult life, and have used the many expressions of art to keep me from jumping into the abyss of no return.

Memories of Life Gone Bye

(Originally written for the "Tall Tale Tell-Off" in Nashville IN, April 2012)

I was at Fort Jackson, South Carolina, for Army Basic Training when I was recruited by the CIA. During that period of time the CIA and the Army were involved in a joint operation. So, I received combined training by both, and it was not easy, there were times I felt like giving up!

I began my double life as a CIA agent and a soldier assigned to military bases in the United States, and various parts the world. My last assignment was to a National Guard military police unit deployed to Iraq. They were to provide security check points with a private contract company called Black Waters. I was there to investigate the spike in National Guard casualties who had been assigned to work with this company.

Black Waters was known to target prior military for employment. During my investigation I found some of these former soldiers had been in military prisons or discharged for various types of misconduct. My mission was to infiltrate Black Waters.

It took five months, but one of their team leaders asked me if I wanted to make a lot of money, paid in cash with no paperwork involved. They wanted a detailed account of the units activities, including all the daily operation schedules not relating to the security check points. Well, I needed the commander and his staffs' help so I revealed who I was, and told them about this group conspiring against them.

In the month that followed, the commander and his staff enjoyed playing cat and mouse with these "renegade mercenary soldiers." With their help the operation went smoothly, and eleven people were brought up on charges.

With my mission complete, I was ready to go home. While preparing for my return trip, I realized that I had found something with this unit, it was a sense of belonging. I was going to miss them. These were real people, you know, the down to earth type, not like what I was used to dealing with. They were even having a "going away" ceremony for me the next day.

At the ceremony I receive a "we love you" plaque and a couple gag gifts. They had even decorated a cake in my honor. I have to say that I was not use to all this sentiment being directed my way.

After the ceremony First Sergeant was lecturing me about the importance of a family, and while he was talking I noticed a man approaching the Commander. He was not wearing a military uniform, and I got that "gut feeling" that something was wrong. Suddenly he shouted, "Here is a gift from Black Waters!"

Everything seemed to move in slow motion in the seconds that followed. First Sergeant and I were tumbling in the air like rag dolls, then motion stopped, and darkness moved in.

I woke up briefly, and the Commander and the First Sergeant was telling me to keep fighting, not to give up, that it wasn't my time yet, and then darkness followed again.

The second time I woke up I felt a sudden jolt of the most intense pain that I have ever experienced. Someone was calling my name, a face was smiling at me. I felt drops of water splashing on me, it was tears coming from that smiling face. Then the face was gone, replaced by the Commander and First Sergeant. The Commander told me that my body was healing that's why I was feeling so much pain, and they would visit to help me take my mind off of it. First Sergeant said I was given an extension on my life, and it was time to start living. The Commander then said that I had a bumpy road ahead of me, but I had it in me to jump over some of those bumps. I suddenly felt very sleepy and before I could tell them goodbye, I was sound asleep.

I had been in and out of a coma for several weeks. The face that I had seen during my brief awakening had been my mother. I was just days from being removed from life support when she saw me open my eyes, it was an answer to her prayers.

It was a rough bumpy road, like the commander had said. I had cuts, fractures and broken bones on my face, arms, hands and legs, plus a fractured skull. The flak jacket that I had been wearing protected my back, neck and ribs, they were only badly bruised. The good news was that my feet were not harmed. Within a month I was moved to a physical therapy center.

Those first few weeks were tough, but my mind was starting to function again. Thoughts and memories were becoming clearer. The casts had been removed, and I was learning to walk again, and to use my arms and hands too.

After the fourth week of physical therapy I started going as an outpatient. I was signing in for outpatient service when I saw one of the soldiers from my last duty assignment in Iraq. He was the first one I had seen besides the Commander and the First Sergeant since the blast. When he saw that it was me, I thought he was going to pass out. I grabbed his arm to steady him, and asked if he needed to sit down.

He looked at me with questioning eyes and said, "You are real aren't you, you're not a ghost!"

I reassured him that I was very much alive, and told him that the Commander and the First Sergeant had come to visit me a few times when I was fighting for my life after the blast. I also told him that if it wasn't for their encouragement I would have given up!

"So they visited you too!" He said with tears in his eyes. He suddenly hugged me and repeated over and over again, "that he wasn't crazy after all."

Well, I was bewildered, and asked him why was he saying that.

He stepped back and looked at me with tears now flowing down his face said, "They both had died in the blast."

Beginning

Its a new beginning, I start to think
Will it be shallow or will it be deep
Will there be a crashing in my soul
Or a release of the pain that's deep and very old
Do I deserve to have joy in my life
Or wish it for others as I see all the strife
It's a new beginning, Oh yes indeed
But I don't think it will ever be for me…

Moments in Time

this is my time…
a time for sorrow… agony
anguish of mind and soul
a time for my character to grow
when the sun is not shinning
and the night has come
when storms rage around me
I hang my head low
fight the tears
then let them flow
when I am alone
this is my time…
there are moments of happiness
to be cherished…
but they are brief moments in time

Mountain True

My heart has plunged into the sea
It's a deep dark sea called Agony
I swim to the surface to get air and light
But Oh! it is becoming such a fight
to swim to the surface because the day is now night
I cry to the mountain to give me stability
I need it to hold on to me
High above it stands so strong and true
I feel its' strength fill me anew
I will make it through the darkness of the night and sea
Because the mountain is there above the sea of Agony

Snap Shot of Life

Sitting on my porch watching the chickens peck and scratch
Kitty comes by for a quick pet on the back
The radio in the background giving the news
A squirrel barks from a tree demanding I take notice from his view

Cloudy morning with a gentle breeze
A car climbs the hill right next to me
Birds all around me singing their song
A chainsaw in the distance humming along

Green colored leaves dancing everywhere
Pink and white flowers enjoying my stare
Buzz buzz goes a bumble bee
Go find a flower and get away from me

The sun peeks through the clouds creating shadows and glow
A Humming Bird flies up to say hello
This is a snap shot of the life that I know

Silently

Love walks silently through
It whispers it's song that can not be sung
As Love walks silently through
I cry out to God to take it away
The sweetness and bitterness is to much to bare
I cry for the feeling to just not care
As the pain and the sorrow weighs heavy on my heart
Free me I pray and give me a new start

The Average Face

I have an average face.
I would get lost in a crowd.
But I have a secret that you can't see if you did look at me.

I am a soldier.
So, big deal! you say to yourself.
I know a soldier, and so does my sister, brother or friend.

The secret is not that I am a soldier.
It is what I have seen
and what I have done being a soldier…

I have seen death standing next to me,
and I have become death to another and another and another…

I once was innocent playing basketball on the court,
but that is a life that I have a hard time remembering.
It's what I have seen, and what I have done
that makes that life a shadow in my past.

Shattered dreams, broken glass, nights awake…
memories haunting…faces haunting…
The faces of those I have killed haunting me in the night.

Faces from a country that I did not know.
Faces from a country that I can not forget.
Shadows on the walls, whispers in the night…

Screaming in my mind, screaming in my dreams…
Screams from a country that I did not know.
Screams from a country that I can not forget.

I have an average face that would get lost in a crowd.
But I have a secret that you can not see if you did look at me.

Death is Not the Enemy

Who would have thought it in that split moment in time...
I'd celebrate with life and wondered secretly why....
I envied death and thought with a sigh...
It will take another who is not yet ready and leave me behind...
I despise the falseness of this human reality...
This human existence and their false values forced on me...
If they could only see what is truth and be set free...
Oh to be free from this body and out of this place...
To soar beyond into outer space....
Why can't they see that death is not the feared enemy...
But a doorway to step through beyond the deep blue sea...
To a world where human blindness is finally gone...
I bet that you think that my thoughts are all wrong...

Ogle Lake, Brown County State Park· © *Jude Edwards*

PEGGY DAILY

Peggy Daily has lived in Brown County for 40 years and is a "naturalized countyian." She wrote the *Practical Women's Guide to Fishing* and is happy to be here and breathing. Her great-grandmother had her own fishing shack on the Wabash River for many years. There are more books in the works and on the way, and Peggy hopes you enjoy all that you read from her.

Root Beer Drinking Coon

While sitting on a lake bank, after cleaning out a casting spot, I got into my cooler for a cold root beer in a can and took a big swig. After sitting it on a flat spot behind me and slightly touching my back, I began casting and reeling to see if the space I made was large enough to keep from getting hung up.

Finally satisfied, I threw out and was watching the bobber as it began to "dance." I was reaching around to grab my can when the bobber went under and away from me. Forgetting the pop, I set the hook and began reeling in my fish; it was big and heavy. Since I was "rocking and reeling," it took a few seconds before I realized a little pressure on my back. Thinking it was my can tipping a little, and expecting it to flip and give me a wet, cold seat, I slowed my rocking, but the pressure was still there.

Getting the fish to the bank, I got it within reach. After removing the fish from the hook, I felt a tap on my shoulder. Expecting to see a C.O., I turned just in time to see a small coon guzzling my root beer from the can and a large coon about 3-inches from my face.

I asked if she wanted the fish, and she turned and chattered something to the smaller coon who used all four feet to flip my can over his head. He stood up to chatter something back at the larger coon who looked at me and seemed to nod. I carefully placed the fish at her feet; she picked it up and took off for the brush.

I guess there are two morals to this story:
1. Be nice to your neighbors.
2. Remember to share.

I went back to the same place several more times when I could and the coon family was always around. Mama coon would scamper up the tree to a limb over-looking my bobber and would let me know when I was about to be blessed with a fish. After I got it to the bank and off the hook, I would lay it down and say "there you go." She would get it and scamper off with one or two little ones behind her.

Fishing is fun!

Dragon

I have a dragon outside my window.
during the day it just looks like a branch on the tree,
but at night it is this dragon that watches over me.

It has been there for only a short time
    in a dragon's life,
but a very long time watching over me.

When I am sick
    I know I'll be fine.
He won't let bad things happen to my mind.

There is a dragon outside my window,
    things will be fine.

Happy Town

A few years ago, Brown County did a "major weed cultivation" of someone's garden in the woods. It took several pick-up trucks to get all of the evidence into town. We had a small police station and jail at that time.

At a loss for what to do with the evidence they could not keep for the trial, they decided to burn it in the high school smoke stack so that it would not get "sampled."

For a few hours everyone was lined up on the street, at first just to watch the "parade" of plant loaded trucks go by, and later to sit in the smoke and enjoy the gift from the police.

Thanks to them, the town was mellow for hours and the restaurants and snack shop did a booming business.

Life

As I sit here with the cat on my lap
    and think about my life and all the animals in it,
I realize how much easier it is to type
    without a cat on your lap,
between your eyes and the keyboard.

But if it is a thing you must do,
I just hope a fly is not bugging too.

You see the thing is,
the fly bothers the cat
as much as the human
and it makes typing a real shaky matter.

Life is like a wardrobe malfunction —
a small flash is worth a lifetime of remembrance!

Becoming a Red Head is Fun

Becoming a red head is probably a decision that most people do not spend days deciding. However, I had lived in this farmhouse for a while and had hair down to my waist and a three year old son. My decision was made in a series of snap judgements. This one day, everyone it seems was pushing my buttons — the neighbors, the son, even the mailman got his two cents in; so, at about 10 AM, it was time. Reading the bottle, it seemed easy — put in on, wait 20 minutes, rinse it out until the water runs clear, you are a red head!

So I began. I got all my long hair covered and waited my 20 minutes, and gathered the stuff I would need to rinse it out — a bucket, a dipper, towels!

How long could it take? Just a quick rinse! But you see I forgot one very important thing, *I could not reach the pump handle by myself.* So after filling my 5-gallon bucket up a few times and dipping the water over my head, I still was not "running clear."

My son, being an inquisitive sort, came upon his mother's plight and was very concerned because there was bright red juice all over the ground, and it was coming from *Mommy's head!*

"Bleeding Mom? You OK? I help."

Not one for taking short answers, I tried to explain, but how? So I started with "would you like to pump for me?"

"Yes," came the excited answer. He got his stool and jumped up on it and grabbed the handle, pulling it down. Water ran and my head was under running water at last. After about five pulls, his stool fell over and he was still holding the pump handle, and we were getting clearer water. And even though I could not see through my hair to him, he was giggling so everything was okay.

By the time I realized that the giggling had stopped, the water was clear and my hair was frozen from the cold water. I got my towel and wrapped up my hair just as another gush of water came pouring out. I don't know how long he had been dangling there, but the whole rinsing out process took about 45 minutes when I finally looked at him. I grabbed him to put him on the ground, and he looked at me with his hands still in pump grabbing position and said, "More," even though his hands were cramped. He had hung on and kicked his feet to get lower and had his own form of seesaw, and it was fun.

After that, it took no time at all the fill the water jugs, all 103 of them for the water in the house, and by then he had had enough fun for one day and declared it was time for lunch and a nap.

Fish Afraid of Water

(This was told to me by a very dear friend.)

A grandfather, son, and grandson went fishing at a nearby lake and were releasing what they caught; all except one fish that lay beside the grandson, who was speaking to it in low tones. Grandfather and father listened for a while, but couldn't make out what was being said.

After about two minutes more, the grandfather said, "You had better put that fish in the water before it dies."

The grandson replied, "It's afraid of the water, Grandpa."

His father started laughing and said, "What kind of fish is afraid of the water?"

"This one is, watch," and with that he picked up the fish and gently put it in the water. It just laid there and did not swim away, it righted itself to look at the boy, but stayed put. The boy picked it back up and placed it on the bank again. It did one flip, turned so he could see the boy and was quiet once more.

The father tried it and got the same results.

"See," the grandson said, "I told ya, he don't like the water!"

Suicide Note

Saturday, June 23, 2012

I committed suicide today, I just thought I would tell you there will be no "body" to find and no funeral to plan but it happened anyway, you can still see my body but I'm not here anymore.

I heard my "life string" twang just a few moments ago; it was the last one holding me here on earth. Sometime two weeks ago my "giggle string" loosened and became a little wobbly, a few days later the "go with the flow" string loosened also. Now I can see the fraying on the end of the "get this done then you can rest string." The "let's be social" string was way to loose for a long time and it made everything sound out of sync anyway. My "get up and go" string was stretched as far as way possible and I think it warped my neck anyway. I was having trouble keeping in tune with my "life" string so when it let go we just all "popped" slowly off. For a few seconds it made a pleasant sound, but that was THE END. Maybe you will see me sitting in the corner, but I won't play any more. When you do see me please remember I was once important in your life and I did make you laugh. Even if I made your fingers ache. With life comes pain, with death comes sorrow, but not for them that never learned to "play well with others." But even though I have played my last note you probably did not hear it. But then again "if a tree falls…"

So how was your week?

The Grace in Stephen's Garden · © Susan W. Showalter

DANA SKIRVIN

Born in Bartlesville, Oklahoma, I have lived in Brown County for only twenty-two years. Fortunately, my husband and children are true Brown-Countians, so much like Jane Goodall, I have been accepted by the locals. With degrees in painting and photography, I go about my business as a masseuse while amassing hundreds of photos 'just because.' Right out of college, I dabbled in group and one woman shows (at the Bellvue, 431 Gallery, The Runcible Spoon, etc.) and had poems in various collections, but over the last fifteen years I've kept pretty much to myself, barefoot and pregnant. Three years ago, I was told that poems die when they are never spoken aloud, so I set out to give my "children" a life of sorts (find each a little one room apartment and a part time job). I participated in poetry readings at Racheals, the county fair, the 2009 Bloomington Cancer Benefit and with W.R.A.P.S. Simultaneously, I've been participating in radio plays with the Figtree Fellowship Radio Players as an actor, play-write and sound effects person. We used my *"Cinderbritches"* script in one of the Brown County Playhouse fund raising events. As for these particular, select poems, I am sending them out into the world because I can't afford to feed them anymore.

An Exhumation

They died in my arms
and I buried them in notebooks,
bits of myself
too tender to look upon.

Broken songs
without breath,
they died
a silent death.

Blowing the dust
from their bare bones,
petrified stones,
I excavate them
as displays of things past
to set behind glass
and get forgotten
again.

Though considered rotten,
they are spoken into life.

Zombie poems,
they come
to suck your brains.

What Game Is This?

I wake before dawn,
nose wrinkled,
hoping that was the dog I smell.
My toes inch across the fuzzy carpet.
A rough fur-lined pad is hastily withdrawn from my path,
confirming my conjecture.

Feeling for his collar, I gently guide him to another room
and close the door between us.

Cowering from the cold of a relentless window fan,
I cover my bare shoulders.

A phrase sounds in my mind.
"I want to play with words."
I smile.

We could play dress-up,
rhyming games and scrabble.
We could create jump rope ditties
and hop through hoops,
looping the words round my tongue
until they're twisted.
"Tag," they say, "You're it."

I reach for a pen or pencil.
I should find one among the small objects perched
    precariously in the openings
that separate my bedroom from the twenty-foot drop into
    my atrium.
This feels more like a game of blind man's bluff than tag.

Walking my fingers along the ledge, I identify
the small, metallic edges of my nail clippers,
the ribbed lid of a jar of Vicks,
the larger, cool slope of my clip-on reading light,

the dusty roughness of wood-be splinters,
a hair band that flips up, rapping my knuckles,
the alternately silky and nappy ear of a stuffed dog,
a pencil,
and the thin edge of a small rectangle
that must be the bookmark my daughter painted for me.

The painted side is gritty from a dried salt peppering its
    surface.
I carefully turn the paper over
and write in straight rows.
I'm hoping the words don't overlap like I've done before,
writing in the dark.

My thoughts thus captured, the game is won.
I drift back to sleep,
paper and pencil still clutched in my hand,
slightly tucked under the corner of my pillow,
safe at home base.

In the morning, I discover my pencil had no lead.
I angle the paper in the light,
searching for deep impressions.

Squirrel Watching

Earthbound,
I wish that I could be
a squirrel away up in a tree.
Whee hee! So free,
a swinging and a swaying in the breeze!

Unless, I dread,
while bounding 'round,
I land on limb that crashes down
and pins me firmly to the ground.
Considered dead and never found…

Dear me.
Rethink this thread.
You'd not be pinned — you would be dead.
The fall alone would crush your head.
'Nuff said.
Earthbound I'll be instead.

Cat Love

My cat and I,
we love each other
and snuggle late
beneath the covers.

I scratch her chin
and stroke her thigh.
She sticks her tail tip
in my eye.

Take Note

They say that life's a song.
Battered by the beat so base,
I race at quickened pace
and labored breath
—no rests—
directly to my death,
the treasured finish line
that lies ahead
(and it does lie).

My measured melody
finds each phrase barred
completely.
When I'm deplete,
my final phase, a slur, to end with double lines,
two lines that cross
could mark a spot of rest
(here lies deceit).
Alas two dots with standing double bars
direct me back again —
I need repeat.

Free-falling Word Folly

I like to roll
free-floating words
around my tongue,
to form flowing poems
from the hawked up emotions
I find flooding
the back of my throat…
yet I fear I am clearly not
fathering pearls of wisdom,
but rather fairly-lovely,
opalescent balls of phlegm.

The Wee Hours

I do enjoy my start of day
with children gone next door to play.
I read a line of verse or two,
sip my tea, and think of you.
Yet as I lift inspired pen,
here come the children home again.

Notes from the Editor

Hillsounds Three, our third W.R.A.P.S. publication, presented me with my first opportunity to edit a book. I quickly accepted this opportunity without giving much thought to what it might be like to work with so many different authors (over twenty!) with widely varying ages and levels of experience. This has been a real learning experience for me and, for that, I am very grateful!

I am particularly happy to have worked on a book which is the first publishing opportunity for many of our W.R.A.P.S. members. I am especially pleased that our book includes some young writers who give all of us older writers a look at life from a different perspective and provide us with a constant source of joy and pride.

I thank all of these authors for their contributions, patience and help to produce *Hillsounds Three.* I especially thank Tess Kean of Two Great Minds. Without her expertise, guidance and patience this book would not have been published.

All of the members of W.R.A.P.S., for the nearly two decades I have attended, have been a great inspiration to me. Many have become close friends. It is my hope that you will also be inspired by their writing.

We invite you to join us at the Brown County Library in Nashville, Indiana any first and third Thursday at 7 PM to listen and share your writing with us. You may also visit us and leave comments for us on our Facebook page — W.R.A.P.S. Happy writing!

— Susan W. Showalter, Editor
Hillsounds Three

Made in the USA
Charleston, SC
20 January 2013